I0575016

Midnight Cumbia

LOVE SONGS FROM DEUS

Midnight Cumbia

4 Horsemen
Publications, Inc.

LYRA R. SAENZ

Midnight Cumbia
Copyright © 2023 Lyra R. Saenz. All rights reserved.

4 Horsemen Publications, Inc.
1497 Main St. Suite 169
Dunedin, FL 34698
4horsemenpublications.com
info@4horsemenpublications.com

Cover by J. Kotick
Typeset by Niki Tantillo
Edited by JM Paquette

All rights to the work within are reserved to the author and publisher. No part of this publication may be reproduced, stored in a retrieval system, or transmitted in any form or by any means, electronic, mechanical, photocopying, recording, scanning, or otherwise, except as permitted under Section 107 or 108 of the 1976 International Copyright Act, without prior written permission except in brief quotations embodied in critical articles and reviews. Please contact either the Publisher or Author to gain permission.

All characters, organizations, and events portrayed in this novel are either products of the author's imagination or are used fictitiously. All brands, quotes, and cited work respectfully belongs to the original rights holders and bear no affiliation to the authors or publisher.

Library of Congress Control Number: 2023934750

Print ISBN: 978-1-64450-929-6
Audio ISBN: 978-1-64450-931-9
Ebook ISBN: 978-1-64450-930-2

Table of Contents

Dedication

To the North Star, who led me to
the smallest love of my life.

Map of Ebele

ORISUMI

100 MILES

Church Bells and Lace

Sometimes a single look will shake a mountain.
Sometimes souls ignite with a spark.
Sometimes it happens as quick as the firing of a bullet.
Sometimes people fall in love.
Other times, they plummet.

A Poem

Cresta De Corail - 27th Day in the Month of Soil

I'VE WORN COUNTLESS DRESSES. *VESTIDOS* upon *vestidos*. All my life, I have been dressed in the finery befitting my station. Beautiful dresses, dresses perfect for the princess of an island country. There were sun dresses and court dresses and temple dresses. There were ceremonial dresses and sailing dresses and afternoon tea dresses. Dresses for every occasion under the sun.

As I grew older, those dresses became gowns, adorned with sparkling diamonds and soft hand-sewn lace. Gowns made from the lightest of silks spun by the palace's specially tended worms. Gowns passed down to me from my mother and grandmother, meant only to be worn once.

Naturally, each gown had to be perfectly paired with a matching set of shoes and the finest pieces of jewelry designed to signify status and grace: a fine tiara once worn by my great-great-grandmother, a pearl necklace and earring set, several fine gemstone circlets to accentuate the colors of my people, sea-harvested gold crafted into delicate bangles and bracelets. Everything I've ever worn was always perfectly chosen to remind any and all who saw me that I was *the* princess of Deriva.

Mamá always made sure of it. Probably in preparation for this day.

This gown is beyond anything I've ever worn before. Layers of taffeta and silk hidden beneath a heavy overskirt, a carefully tailored bodice designed both to accentuate certain assets and provide modesty, and the weight of what must be thousands of ocean-harvested gemstones: all these things compound to make this one gown. A gown which will never be worn again, not by me, not even by any daughters I may or may not have.

"Oh, Atzi, can you believe it? Today's the day!"

Mamá hovers behind me, her hands resting warm on my bare shoulders. Our eyes meet in the mirror. I always wished I'd gotten my mother's eyes. Not that I hate my own golden browns, but the Vulcana's rich hazel is such a unique shade here in the isles. Most everyone here has brown eyes. Mamá is the only person I've ever known to have eyes that weren't brown, well with the exception of my sister and her mother, but their eyes aren't hazel.

Mamá's eyes sparkle, looking more green against the color of her gown. I've never seen her so happy. I try not to wince as a bobby pin pokes into my scalp when Mamá affixes the seemingly miles-long veil to the crown of my head.

She lets it go to drape over my shoulders, and my goddess, it's so heavy I feel like I've lost a whole inch off my height.

Church Bells And Lace

"This is the veil I wore the day I married your father. My mother fixed it into my hair just like this."

"It's beautiful, Mamá," I say, adjusting the angle of my head and trying to lengthen my neck to avoid the headache I know this veil will pry out of the depths of my skull after the required three hours of the ceremony.

I should be more grateful. It really is a beautiful veil. It falls in splendid cascades around my shoulders, a drapery of sheer blue *malines* lace edged in gorgeous gold rosettes of coral and dotted with aquamarine crystals and pearls.

Instead, I can't get past the stranger staring back at me in the mirror.

Her eyelashes are much longer and thicker than mine. The cosmetic-enhancement augmentation Mamá had my doctors install last week is doing its work, polishing and hardening this stranger's nails by increasing the amount of keratin in her system. The augmentation channels color into the skin of her face by directing the blood to pooling into just the right capillaries to accentuate the high curve of her cheekbones and diminish the width of her jawline. ("You have your father's cursed jowls." Mamá used to always say that before caking on a smattering of bronzer to hide the strength in my chin.) The augmentation even enhances the sparkle of the other woman's eyes by making her tear ducts emit minute amounts of water.

On top of all that, one of the finest beauticians has made her up today. A dusting of gloss over her lips makes them sparkle in the light, a touch of eyeliner makes her eyes appear wider, and a thin splash of highlight under her eyes makes her cheekbones all the more enticing. If the make-up wasn't enough, gems have been adhered to the thin line of her brow. A pair of diamonds rests daintily on her lashes.

This is not my face, and yet, it is.

The augmentation isn't Derivan technology. The tech of my homeland is not so intricate nor so biological. This is Ebelean tech, which means it will soon be my tech.

You would think, considering the extravagance of my dress, that such decorations would be moot, yet here I am, unable to recognize my own face in the mirror. The servants and planners and palace staff have me all dolled up for the world to see, and no, that is not a hyperbole.

"Atzi, my darling, the cameras are going to just love you. You'll be an inspiration to young girls all over Deriva. In fact, I bet they'll be making dresses inspired by yours all across Deus."

In just a few short moments, I'll be walking out of the door of this little bridal boudoir straight into the lens of a camera. My maid will slip a pair of light-blocking goggles over my eyes, and Papá will escort me into the carriage that'll drive us to the cathedral, Ueyachantli. In stepping into that carriage, I will be saying goodbye to Cresta de Corail, the place where I was born.

Mamá smooths the edges of the veil and fusses with a few invisible strands of hair that aren't actually out of place. There are tears at the edges of my mother's eyes. Of course, there are. Her daughter is getting married. I've never seen Mamá cry, but I guess, if there was going to be a day for tears, it would be today.

"I can't tell you how proud I am of you. This is the biggest day of your life. Everything is going to be just perfect!"

"Gracias, Mamá."

As easily as the Vulcana's smile comes, it disappears as my baby sister enters the room. It's no wonder why, really. For all that my gown has been meticulously designed and styled to showcase my status as the "sole" princess of Deriva, Wren's dress was carefully picked to highlight her newly acquired status as a technomancer, more so, of course, than her role as maid of honor in the day's festivities.

The dark blue silk of the skirt is accented by an asymmetrically tailed, black, cotton bodice. The collar line circles around her shoulders to cave into a hood. Wren's long raven-dark curls shine blue as they cascade from the hood of the bodice. There are some fine details throughout, lace details and hand-sewn swatches of needle lace and beading shaped in the same motifs found in the lace of my gown.

And like a shining badge of her achievements, Mångata hangs from a soft leather belt at Wren's hip. The aetherkalis, even in sleep, speaks louder than anything as to my sister's worth. Just let the public shame her ever again for being the daughter of a Firefly. I dare them.

"Oh, Atzi, you look beautiful."

Wren's smile is infectious in the best possible way. My baby sister, all of sixteen and holding more status than most people could even dream of, is a beautiful badass.

"Only because I have the best maid of honor," I singsong back, holding my hands out for Wren to take. She does, of course, giving my gloved palms a squeeze.

"Last I checked, hoods were not the current fashion for bridal parties. Really, Atzi, I can't believe you let her choose such a dress."

"Wren is a technomancer, Mamá. Her gown should reflect her status, not hide it. Besides, I quite like the hood."

Especially, considering I'm the one who added said addition.

I wink at Wren, who merely shrugs. Sad to say, she is plenty used to my mother's constant exasperation. She's only been drawing it since the day she was born. Wren has a pretty colorful way of describing it. Something about there being a reason Freya didn't have Wren in the hospital because she's "pretty sure Elisabeta would have made sure I got switched with another baby."

Elisabeta's ire, however, is misdirected anyway. Wren had very few opinions about the overall look of her attire. I actually designed the whole ensemble. I wanted my sister to wear something useful. Corvo even made the bodice to come apart, with black, woven leathers bracing each of the stays, making it a perfect piece of armor for whenever Wren decided to take it out to the field. I had it specially made for my sister as a graduation gift of sorts, one both useful in combat and fitting for courtly festivities. It was the project that saved my sanity through the last few months. It's been a whirlwind of wedding planning since Chike "earned his stripes," as it were.

I turn to Wren.

"Is Papá alright? The last I saw him, he was sweating bullets and having trouble with his sash."

"He's fine. Just excited. Do you need any adjustments before your call?"

"You fit me in this so perfectly, I don't even want to risk going to the bathroom."

Mamá makes a strange keening sound in what I assume to be snub at Wren.

"I'm sure Maria would be quite displeased to hear all of her hard work being chalked up to your sister. How do you think such a lack of care reflects on you, Atzi?"

Maria is my sister and my shared maid, though I suppose with Wren's promotion and the main festivities in occurrence today, the appropriate tense is now "was."

"Maria knows how much I'll miss her."

For the last five years, Maria has been our shared dresser, the maintainer of our rooms and clothing, and our lady escort on shopping trips into town. Since Wren's shift in status, Maria has been solely in my service, helping plan this wedding, acting as a confidante, signing and sealing hundreds of invitations and correspondences between diplomats and dignitaries, flower shops and caterers, dress shops and shoe shops, and tailors and decorators. Anything and everything you can think of, Maria helped me figure out. Never mind that there was a small battalion of wedding planners also working on this extravagant affair, but Maria is my dearest *dama* and probably the only person who actually asked for my opinion on any of the decisions.

However, now that I will be undertaking the role of a married woman, Maria's duties are finished. Once I am set up in my husband's household, it'll be some stranger waking me in the morning, pressing my dresses, and buttoning my bodice.

It's a bit unfair of Elisabeta to make such a point now simply to spite Wren, who has been helping Maria all day. She could have very easily left countless other servants to assist in the process of dressing the bride-to-be, but Xochtli knows Wren's strength augmentations made touting the wedding dress across the room a hell of a lot easier.

"That's right, Atzi!" trills Wren. "How could you forget all of the last-minute tailoring Maria had to do last night because Corvo made the mistake of not putting in a bustle?!"

I laugh. Wren's trademark sarcasm, even when aimed at my mother, always serves as a better weapon than any blade.

"Your majesty?"

The head wedding planner pokes his head into the room.

"What?" snaps Elisabeta.

"We are in need of our Vulcana at the southern awning. You are scheduled now for pictures with his majesty."

"That's now?"

"Yes, ma'am. And the bride-to-be should be ready to go soon as well."

"How soon?"

The man checks his watch.

"Twenty minutes before the carriage is scheduled to depart, ma'am."

Elisabeta huffs, turning from Atzi in favor of fixing her own gown.

"Very well. I'm on my way. Atzi, my dear, don't be late. The public waits for no one."

"Yes, Mamá."

Elisabeta curves around the planner and disappears out the door.

"Princess, you've got about five more minutes before father-daughter photos. Then we have to do mother-daughter, siblings, and bridesmaids. If we have time, I would like to fit in groomsmen and—"

"Thank you, Corvo. I'll have her out in just a moment," snips Wren, all but shutting the door in the man's face. "I think we've got the picture."

The door clicks shut, and suddenly, the weight of the day clamps down on my shoulders, and I'm fairly certain my hair would have wilted were it not for the copious amounts of hairspray currently keeping it from giving in to gravity. So, instead of letting my hair fall, I do. My knees buckle as easily as a newborn calf's until I'm little more than a head sticking out of a puddle of fabric on the display step.

"Is it over yet?"

"I'm afraid it hasn't even really started, love."

Wren shuffles her way over to where I'm settled on the floor.

"I don't think I can do this."

"Want me to stow you away? I could, you know. We'll bundle you up in one of the sea skimmers and make our way to the mainland. We can change our names, dye our hair, and escape into the wilds where no one will ever find us. We'll even drag Xipilli along, too. Got to get our entertainment from somewhere since there won't be internet service anywhere."

The chuckle bubbles up and a little bit of the weight lifts.

"I have to do this."

"Yes, *mi hermana*, but do you want to do this?"

"In some ways, yes. In other ways, maybe. I just... everything is going to change, and I don't know how to keep up."

I don't even believe my own words. I doubt Wren does. Even so, she doesn't say anything for a few minutes. She simply looks at me, softly, in the mirror, her eyes the color of the shallow waters around the coral reefs that circle her villa.

I wonder what color the waters are in Ebele. I know the great savannah that comprises half the continent is infamous for its dry season. Even the major rivers dwindle down so low the crocodiles can barely keep themselves submerged, their cute noses sticking out of the water like floating buttons. But

Chiamaka told me, in contrast, that in the wet season, the rivers overflow, the shoreline retreating so far back, sometimes the local villagers need to activate the high-rise legs embedded under their homes to elevate their houses above the flood line.

Eventually, Wren comes to kneel next to me.

"I'm glad her majesty was called away because I'm fairly certain she would have my head for poaching this for you before your wedding ceremony, but I figure we can always touch up your lipstick later."

Like magic, Wren pulls out a wonderfully sweet-smelling, flaky, sugar-coated churro. My favorite sweet snack.

"Where did you...?"

"I had Maria do me one last favor. You know she always makes them the best from scratch."

"Is there—"

"Icing?" In her other hand appears a warm cup of beautifully melted frosting. "Of course, there is. Do you think I would forget that my sister takes her churros with extra glucose for some ungodly reason?"

Wren decorates my front with what feels like another dress of napkins before handing over the treat. It's warm to the touch and sticky with sugar and cinnamon, just the way they should be. People say the best churros are bought from the street vendors in downtown Mareatierra. They make them fresh in a pot of oil after blending the batter from scratch, but that's not the impressive part. It's what comes after they've finished frying the churros. You would not believe the extra mile these chefs will go to sugar the churros. The best ones turn it into a right dance of sugar and cinnamon.

But they've never had a churro made by Maria. Her father owned a food truck.

"Wren, you're a pill."

"Now I'm going to go guard the door so you can eat in peace and quiet. When you're ready to go, just page me, and we'll get you over to your next appointment wherever or whenever that may be."

"We have a schedule to keep, Wren."

"Yeah, and the last I checked, no wedding ever took place without at least both consenting parties being present. If my bride needs a few extra minutes, then this maid of honor is going to make sure she gets them, damnit."

"How did I get blessed with such a sister?"

"I don't know. Ask your dad 'cause your mom had nothing to do with it."

The joke is utterly inappropriate, yet still my sister manages to make me smile. However, I must shoot her a "shame on you" pointing of my finger for good measure. Not that she sees it. The girl is already walking out the door, one hand on her weapon as though ready to slice down any person who might disturb my date with this churro.

Goddesses, I love that girl. I'm going to miss her.

The first bite of the churro is divine. It has the perfect amount of crunch with soft, gooey innards. As per usual, Maria topped it with the perfect amount of cinnamon and sugar.

This is the first time I've been left all alone all day. Maria woke me up at six, and ever since, I've been bathed, pampered, fluffed up, and powdered by so many different people I couldn't tell you any of their names if my life depended on it. On top of that, I didn't really get much sleep last night. Too many butterflies fluttering around in my stomach. I spent the night tossing and turning so badly, I forced myself to go for a walk in an attempt to rid myself of some of the pent-up energy. Somehow my feet carried me to the kitchens for a warm cup of goat's milk.

The intention had been to sneak down and sneak back up without disturbing anybody. Naturally, all the best intentions are for nothing. I got down to the kitchen to find Xipilli already there himself.

"Hola, hermano."

"Atzi, what are you doing up?"

"I couldn't sleep."

Without another word, my little brother got up from his seat and made me a mug of perfectly tempered milk, complete with a few sprigs of vanilla and a sprinkling of cinnamon.

"Talk to me. What's wrong?"

His question unleashed a flood of tears. They fell as rain from the clouds of doubt, anxiety, and fear lingering in my heart. *What if Chike never loves me? What if I never figure out how to love him? What if we end up like my parents: co-existing out of obligation rather than any true desire for companionship? What if I become just like Mamá, bitter because the husband she married fell in love with another woman?*

I can't become my mother. I love her, dearly. Really, I do, but I'm not strong like she is. I'm no technomancer. I'm not strong like her. If Chike chose to love another woman... I don't know if I could survive being married to someone who didn't love me.

Xipilli listened quietly, unbothered by the fact that tears were soaking into his pajama top. It was unfair really. Why should he have to listen to me cry in the middle of the night? I'm the eldest. I should be supporting him. I should have been the one cheering him on as he began his tenure as a technomancer. I should have been working to support him in any way I could think of now that he had been named heir apparent to the throne of Deriva. I should have been letting his tears soak into my nightgown as he lamented the loss of his youth, stressed over the missions to come, confided in him about the fear for every danger he was set to face over the next handful of years.

And to top it all off, there I was crying over marrying his best friend. I cried about making his favorite person in life his brother-in-law. Talk about selfish.

"Ya know, Chike had better be thankful for you because I can't think of a better person for him to call his bride, Atzi."

I blinked at him.

"I'm not supposed to tell you this, but Chike is just as nervous as you are."

"What? Why would he be nervous?"

"Don't know, but his stag weekend was less of a party and more of a try-to-get-Chike-to -relax-enough-to-eat-something-so-he-doesn't-starve-himself-to-death-before-the-wedding."

"That can't be true."

"It's true, Atzi. And he was a weepy mess, too. Burbling on and on about how he was going to disappoint you. How unfair it was that you were the one having to marry a younger man and not he a younger woman. You could have filled the Pacificum with that vato's tears. For a second, I thought I was going to have to knock him unconscious to get him down the aisle. I tell you, Atzi. Make sure you have a good lady's maid because the number of hankies you're going to need cleaned on the daily... Whew! I don't envy your laundry units."

That was when I really and truly laughed. A good long laugh that felt like the sun dancing over the horizon. That laugh is probably still carrying me through today. Well, that and the next thing my brother said.

"And I swear it, Atzi. If he so much as makes you cry even once, I'll give him the worst hell he could ever imagine."

I can't help but smile about the recent memory as I munch on my churro.

I couldn't have asked for a better set of siblings. My sister scalping me something from the kitchens to grant me just a moment of peace while my brother's words nest in my heart like a baby bird. If there is anything I'm going to miss here in Cresta de Corail, it's going to be my siblings.

I don't think I could have ever survived this circus called life without them. How am I supposed to manage living in a completely different country without either of them at my side?

There's sugar everywhere, but Wren did a hell of a job making me a bib of napkins. I'm cautious as I remove them before I make my way back to standing. The dress falls back in place as smoothly as ever, as though I hadn't just sat myself down in the middle of all those layers and layers of skirts.

And there are many, many layers under that top skirt.

My mother chose a full ball gown dyed in the palest of blues. The fabric of the skirt, a wonderfully light chiffon, is shelled and folded to lay in a mimicry of the scales of one of the sea's most majestic creatures: a marlin. The pieces bundle and fold low around my hips as the bodice begins, rising up to caress every curve of my torso like a gentle wave. Where most dresses are donned with lace in extravagant floral patterns, the lace of my gown has been lovingly woven with coral and seaside motifs: shells, anemones, pearls, cup and fire coral, seahorses, and starfish.

The veil my mother pinned to my head is a more vibrant silk, treated with a beautiful azul dye and embroidered with gold thread. It drapes around me as a homage to my people's heritage while a hanging tiara of gems holds it in place. The island peoples of Deriva have always had a love for fine fabrics in bright colors: pinks, oranges, blues, purples, and greens.

It really is a beautiful gown. So beautiful it is that this day will be the only day I'll ever wear it. This day, my wedding day, is the last day I will be Princess Atzi Moctezumo of Deriva. 'Tis the true burden of being born a girl of the aristocracy. You spend your whole life learning how to live inside of one identity, only to have it all stripped away so you can fulfill your true purpose.

Once all the ceremonies are done and the vows are spoken, I will no longer be the princess of Deriva. I will become Princess Atzi Naga of Ebele, a foreign princess of a strange land.

Never again will I be the princess of the islands I've always called home.

2

Bossa Nova

U EYACHANTLI, OUR BEAUTIFUL
TEMPLE, has been decorated just for me with vines of
lilies and strings of lights, hung tapestries and draperies. As
a wedding of royal stature, the cathedral is filled to capacity
with dignitaries and foreign aristocrats. Outside the sanc-
tity of my green room, there are probably over a hundred
people sitting in the cathedral's ring of seats. On the other
side of the cameras, there are thousands watching this event
live. Ueyachantli is the old nahuatl word for Ocean Home. It's
always kind of been like that for us. A home away from home
for the people of the sea.

Today, it feels less like a home and more like an arena.

Weddings always used to make me cry. The first wedding
I ever attended was Papá's to Freya Nocturne.

I hadn't met the woman yet. All I knew of her were the
whispers that followed her name down the hall and the dis-
gust with which Mamá mentioned "that other woman."

Yet when I finally met her, I couldn't understand why so
many people said such bad things about her.

I remember it so clearly, the first time I met her.

It was on a Saturday. I was a flower girl. The flowers had been the beautiful shades of lavender and peony blue. My nursemaid had led me from my bedroom, where they'd fixed up my hair and done some light make-up on my cheekbones, to the boudoir that would become Freya's chambers once her marriage to my father was finalized.

Freya was the most beautiful woman I had ever seen. That feels like a terrible thing to say. Shouldn't my mother be the most beautiful woman in my life? And she was, really. My mother is a goddess given mortality. She is strong and wise, fierce and protective, like Hestia, Hera, or Athena. She would loathe being described as an Aphrodite. Beauty and love are simply not in her temperament. "Wasteful things, Atzi. Wasteful things."

My dress was a perfect replica of the bride's dress, save for the petals hand-sewn into my skirt. Freya had sewn them in herself. I know because I watched her add the final touches to my dress while she sat in her own wedding gown, which, now that I think on it, wasn't nearly as extravagant as mine today on my own wedding day. Freya wore a simple empire-waisted shift tied with a simple blue sash. The train trailed probably no more than four or five feet behind her, and she hadn't bothered with a veil, choosing instead to honor her heritage with a crown of flowers and crystal set atop an ornate design of braids and knots in her long, pale hair. At her hip, she carried an old sword.

I remember asking her why she was carrying a weapon. Only technomancers carry blades around, and what need did a Firefly have for a sword? She laughed, a beautiful musical laugh that made me ever more enchanted by her, then she lifted me into her lap—I remember this very clearly because one of her dressers just about had a panic attack at the prospect of a toddler wrinkling the Vulcan's soon-to-be-bride's dress—and explained that in her culture, the sword was a vital part of a wedding ceremony.

BOSSA NOVA

"In the elder days, before the moons ever circled Deus as they do now, swords were not so much symbols of power, worn only by the privileged few. A sword is for anyone with something to protect. In my homeland, it is customary for the bride and groom to exchange weapons. It is a symbolic transfer of protection from one family to another, but even more so, it is the promise between lovers to forever protect the love they share for one another."

Naturally, being a princess, I'd been exposed to happily-ever-after fairy tales where the prince slays the dragon, the princess finds her lost slipper, and the villain disappears into the dust from whence they came. But this idea of both a prince and princess fighting for their place in the world... It was so terribly romantic.

In all my two-year-old wisdom, I decided, in that moment, that I would love Freya like a second mother, and in a lot of ways, Freya was exactly that to me.

She then threaded her fingers through my carefully braided hair and presented my flower girl dress to my nurse-maid. I giggled and laughed as Freya cheered me on for every twirl and spin I made as I danced around her boudoir. She let me dance around her right up until my nurse took me away. As the flower girl, it was my job to escort Papá down the aisle.

It was a small ceremony. Papá held my hand down the decorated dock and onto the small gondola where he would give his vows to Freya. On the shore, a handful of chairs were situated, bearing some of Papá's closest friends and a few Fireflies whom Freya considered family.

The officiant had been one of the madams from L'amor Lux. I sat with my nurse once Papá had been safely escorted to the head of the gondola.

Mamá didn't attend.

I didn't know why at the time. I wouldn't know until I was quite a bit older. It was because Mamá was angry. She was angry that my father had fallen so in love with another woman that he decided to marry her, a Firefly who was supposed to take a vow of solitude in deference to her station.

But I didn't know any of this at the time. All I knew was that the villa had been decorated with the most beautiful of flowers, and Papá, a man wrinkled with the weight of a thousand people's lives at just thirty years of age, looked like the happiest man alive when he saw Freya walking toward him from across the dock.

I wonder what Chike will look like as I walk toward him. Is it even possible for a man to be happy when his chosen bride was picked not by him but by political negotiations?

Wren dabs a handkerchief under my eyelashes.

"Oh, Atzi, don't do that. You'll ruin your make-up."

"If a few tears ruin her make-up, then I'll be sure to not only fire the make-up artist but make sure she never finds work in cosmetology again."

"Of course, Xipilli, because a smear of eyeliner is worthy of being banished from an entire career field."

They are gathered around me in the back wing of the cathedral, my green room as it were. My whole half of the bridal party is here with me. I can hear the music starting outside. Soon enough, Chiamaka will be heading down the aisle with Absko to greet Chike waiting with the priest at the altar. They aren't here, the Ebelean party being held elsewhere, but at exactly one minute and three seconds, the planner will cue them to march and the entire debacle will begin.

"This is a royal wedding. There are standards to be upheld, and if the damned make-up artist can't meet them, then she should find a different career path, perhaps that of painting pictures on children's faces at the carnival."

"Xipilli, there is no need to snub someone for an offense they haven't even committed yet." A new, deeper voice enters the middle of my siblings' latest dispute. This is one I haven't heard all day.

"Papá," I say.

BOSSA NOVA

Tlanextli Moctezumo is probably one of the most handsome men in the world. Tall as a volcano, dark and strong and unshaking, this is the man who picked me up off the docks the first time I skinned my knee. He had been teaching me how to ride a bicycle. This is the man who showed me that honor was not only in the sword but in the voice, in the words we choose to use and the ones we leave unsaid. Even with the scarring around his eye and roughness of his hands, never before was there a man more worthy of the title Vulcan as my papá. But even better than the strength of his presence is how warm his hugs are.

"Atzi, my darling!"

I'm all of five years old again as he wraps me in his arms.

"You are the most beautiful sight these sore eyes have ever seen."

"Thank you, Papá."

"Are you ready?"

A knot forms in my throat, so all I can do is shake my head no.

"Sweetheart, you will be fine," hushes my mother. "I remember my wedding day like it was yesterday. I was nervous just like you are, but my mother reminded me as I am about to remind you: Once you reach that altar, the temple priestesses will guide you and Chike into marriage. All you'll have to do is follow along."

My mother gives me one last hug before holding her hand out to my brother.

"Xipilli, come. It's time. Wren, once we are halfway down, you will come through on your own." She steps through the curtain blocking the doorway, tugging Xipilli along before adding over her shoulder. "Don't forget to light up Mångata."

"Sí, Mamá," drawls Wren. She circles her arms around my neck one last time. "See you on the other side of the wedding march, sis." She plants a kiss on my cheek and then follows behind Elisabeta and Xipilli, leaving me alone with my father.

"Papá…"

"My little raindrop."

"How am I going to do this?"

The man's face softens with sorrow. Even his eyes, as dark as they are already, dim at my question.

"Do not think of this as a hurdle to be overcome, Atzi. Think of this as the beginning of a new adventure."

"Is that what your marriage is to Mamá? A grand adventure?"

"Your mother and I are two very different people, Atzi, but that doesn't mean we don't love each other."

"But you fell in love with Freya."

"Is the heart such a confined space that there is only enough room for one other within it?"

I don't know how to answer that question, so Mamá's words to me the night I found out I was betrothed bubble up to answer for me.

"Atzi, dear. You do not love Chike, and Chike does not love you. While I might hope that such truths will change with time, I will not pray for such foolish things as love to blossom between you and your betrothed."

"Mamá, how could you expect me to marry someone I don't love?"

"I married your father, didn't I?"

"I thought you loved him."

Elisabeta laughs.

"Yes, and in return, he fell in love with a Firefly. Love has got about as much to do with marriage as hatred has to do with war. You will marry. You will have your first child, and then Chike, in all his masculine wisdom, will fall in love with someone else, thus giving you the freedom to do as you please."

"Then why would you damn me to such a fate?"

"Because better than the love of any man is the power of a royal seat. Better than the comfort of any sentiment is the solidarity of having a place in this world. That is what this marriage to Chike will bring you. The insurance of a crown and the autonomy to live your life however you see fit. Polygamy is outlawed in Ebele, so at

least you'll not suffer the same humiliation I did when your father saw fit to marry that concubine."

"But it doesn't do that..." I wanted to say back then, even though I didn't have the words to do so.

"Mamá certainly seems to think so."

Papá sighs. "I know she does, but that doesn't make her right." He comes to sit next to me on the settee.

"Atzi, if what your mother says is true, and the heart is only big enough to love one person at a time, then explain to me how, the moment you were born, I thought I would burst with the love that filled my whole being? How is it that my heart grew even larger when your brother came into this world? How could Freya have become such an important part of my life if my heart could not accommodate her? How could your mamá, who has been by my side through war and peace, through life and death, through loss and celebration, still be as vital and integral to my life if I didn't love her?"

"I never thought about it that way."

"There are few who would, but Atzi," my father sets his hands on my shoulders, "regardless of what verdict your hearts eventually come to, whether you grow in love, in friendship, or simply in coexistence, your papá will be there to guide you through the best and the worst parts of it. I promise you this."

My vision blurs around the edges, my face gets warmer, and it gets harder to swallow as the tears finally spill over.

"Oh, Papá!"

I sob into his jacket. It's so awful what I am doing. I'm going to stain his suit and right before he walks me down the aisle, but he doesn't seem bothered.

"Shh, my raindrop. I've got you. I've got you." His big hands are warm as they rub my back.

"Your majesty, it is your cue!"

The damned wedding planner sticks his whole head into the green room without even knocking.

"We need five more minutes, Corvo."

"But my liege—"

"I said five more minutes."

Papá's command leaves no room for argument. The slighter man gives an undignified *meep* and disappears. It's funny enough to merit a small chuckle from me. I can vaguely hear him commanding the orchestra to kill time with another refrain before my music begins.

"I don't know if I can do this, Papá."

"You can, and you will. You are so much stronger than your mother gives you credit for, Atzi. In fact," he leans toward me conspiratorially, "I would even venture to say that, despite all the pomp and circumstance surrounding your brother's and sister's success, you are twice as strong as they are. You have always been. How else could they have managed without the guiding hand of a big sister like you?"

The smile tugs at my mouth, and somehow, everything feels a little easier.

"Come. It is time."

He takes my hand, and we rise together as the music beyond my small palace of draperies shifts.

Ueyachantli means Ocean Home.

I feel like I am drowning as I make my way down the congregation. Everyone has risen for my entrance. Papá is a solid pillar next to me, our steps in sync with one another as the music rises in delicate spirals around the temple. My mother, in the front row, is crying. She dabs at her eyes with a handkerchief, gesturing back every so often for a new hanky from her lady-in-waiting. At the altar, my sister stands as my maid of honor and protector with Mångata lit before her, a sign that, should the groom leave Deriva's princess wanting, the people of the isles will not suffer such an insult without bloodshed. It's symbolic, of course, but meaningful anyway. I know she wouldn't hesitate to take off my groom's head if he did, in fact, decide to humiliate me. Next to her is Chiamaka, looking stunning in the fiery bridesmaid gown I designed for her. Xipilli is on the groom's side of things. As best man, he too has donned his weapon, but Opactli is quiet, inactive in a show of peace and good will.

Lastly is Chike, handsome in his own wedding attire of orange and red. There's a small smile on his face, but I don't dare meet his eyes. Not yet. Not until I absolutely have to.

When I reach the altar, our fathers exchange handshakes, and Chike offers me his palms. I accept his invitation, my bouquet shared between our fingers.

"You look beautiful, Atzi."

Our eyes meet, and it is reassuring to know that tears glimmer in his eyes just like mine. Suddenly, I don't feel as horribly alone.

3

Serengeti Dreams

"It is not a lack of love, but a lack of friendship that makes unhappy marriages."

Friedrich Nietzsche, 1844-1900 A.D.,
German philosopher

One Week Later - Orisumi, Ebele

"YOUR HIGHNESS, I'VE LAID OUT your garments for the day."

Maria's voice is hushed in the darkness. I hear her rustling around, making her way to the windows. Before the reception was over, I offered Maria a job as my lady's maid here in Orisumi. She said yes without a second thought, and I couldn't have been happier.

A few seconds later, light sears the insides of my eyelids. Okay, maybe "sears" is too strong of a word. I'm simply unused to waking up to sunlight. My windows back home face west. The windows of my new quarters face east which means, *"Buenos dias"* comes with a nice bright wake-up call.

My shoulders pop as I stretch my arms over my head.

My personal rooms are as lavish as can be expected for the wife of the heir to the throne, but for some reason I don't understand, I was expecting something different. I'm not sure what I was expecting, but it wasn't my own room separate from my husband.

Even my parents have a conjoined set of rooms. Their royal suite is set up to where they each have their own bedroom and their own sitting room, separated by a shared lounge where they can eat together. Mamá keeps her doors closed so often, it's easy to forget that Papá's room is just a breezeway away.

My suite is on the far side of the compound from Chike's.

I'm not sure if I should feel snubbed by this or if there is some greater reasoning behind it all. I don't know, and I don't dare ask. I've only been here for a day. Chike and I spent our wedding night off the Derivan coastline, our nuptials concluding with a farewell toast as we boarded the private yacht that would sail us to Ebele's borders.

The few days aboard our private little vessel had been nerve-wrecking and exhilarating at once. Nerve-wrecking for exactly the reason you might imagine. Exhilarating for exactly not the reason you might imagine. Chike and I did consummate our marriage on our wedding night. Two virgins fumbling around in the dark, not because we wanted to fiddle with each other, but because it was our duty to do so.

After that, however, we spent more of our time whale watching and enjoying the sights as we passed by some of the greatest ports in Deus. That was the exhilarating part. Chike wanted to make sure I had a good time, so he showed me all over Ebele's coast. We got to see herds of elephants, pods of dolphins, and schools of hammerhead sharks.

"*Princesa, es tu hermana llamando.*"

"*Gracias, Maria. Lo tomaré en mi sala. ¿Puedes volver para ayudarme a vestirme en unos diez minutos?*"

"*Sí, Señora.*"

Maria bows and makes her way out of the room.

SERENGETI DREAMS

I slide out of bed and make my way into the *sala*. Chike has ensured my access to every creature comfort that could be afforded someone in today's world. A sleek, brass-plated computer sits on the surface of an ornate bamboo desk, its motherboard woven into the very furniture to reduce the running of cables and clutter. It's much larger than any system I've ever worked with; my inclinations always geared towards handheld tablets and laptop computers when needed. Xipilli and Wren were always the ones more inclined to sitting at a pseudo-supercomputer. I much prefer something smaller and handheld. I can't be sure how much I'll use it, but I suppose now that I'm so far away from my family, it'll be nice to have a way to video call them whenever I'd like.

Right now, the monitor is alight and buzzing with the incoming call. Wren's screen name flashes at the center of the screen.

It takes me a second to figure out how to operate the holographic keyboard, but with a quick flick across the ENTER key, the screen opens, filled with the image of Wren's face.

"Atzi!"

"Hey, Wren! Burned down the villa yet?"

"Ha, ha... Your confidence in me is astonishing."

"Call it faith, *hermana*."

"Well, I'll have you know that not only have I managed to behave, but I also just accepted my first off-island mission."

"That's amazing! *¿Adónde vas?*"

"Xipilli and I are going to Lorelei."

"Lorelei? But that's a neutral zone."

"Yeah, I'm not too clear on it either, but someone's apparently been causing trouble in the area. A few adepts have gone missing there in the last few weeks, and apparently a technomancer went offline when he went to investigate, so they are sending a team of technomancers to investigate."

"So, you and Xipilli are tackling it together?"

"Yup, though I think Papá said two Murasakan technomancers would also be joining us."

Two technomancers from Murasaki no Yama... How interesting. Especially considering a certain someone my sister just couldn't help but mention every thirty minutes or so.

"Oh, any idea who those two technomancers will be?"

"Not a clue, not a care. It hardly matters who else is assigned because I fully intend to solve this case myself. Xipilli and I are already running a betting pool on who will catch the culprit first."

I laugh. "And I'm sure that plan won't change even in the slightest should one of the Murasakan technomancers be, oh, I don't know, one Kaito Miyazaki."

Wren's cheeks go pink.

"Of course, it wouldn't. Why would anything change just because he's there?"

"You mean you wouldn't be happy to see him?"

"Why should I be happy to see that monosyllabic arse?"

"I don't know... You did say you had a nice time dancing with him on the rooftop."

"You fiend! You promised me you would never bring that up again."

I laugh into my palm.

"I just thought maybe your opinion of him might have changed as a result."

Wren crosses her arms with a harrumph. "He is the epitome of regulation and decorum. Utterly boring and infuriating in equal measure. His only saving grace is how easily flustered he gets at the slightest joke against his person. As handsome as he is, he would put a whole damper on the entire mission. Though I will admit it would probably be nice to get another one-up on him. Not that any of my opinion really matters because I'm pretty sure he hates my guts. I am, after all, eternally 'troublesome.'"

Wren rolls her eyes and looks at the camera sidelong.

"But enough about me. Let's talk about you, Mrs. Nagi."

Wren's eyes narrow, and her trademark smile turns to a lopsided smirk. Uh oh... I know that look, and I've learned to approach that look with extreme caution. "Wren, I swear if you—"

"Soooo, how was it?"

My cheeks go hot. I'm not going to pretend I don't know what she's asking about, but I'm going to pretend I don't know what she's talking about.

"How was what?"

"You know. Your wedding night. How was it? Did you have a chance to try that tea I gave you?"

"Wren, I highly doubt anything I have to say on the matter would be of interest to you. Why don't you go and read one of those awfully smutty novels you like so much?"

"This coming from the girl who used to sneak my mom's books into her room because she had a huge crush on—what was his name again—King Ragnar of the Icey Mar."

"Wren!"

Damned technomancer memory drives. There's nothing my sister ever forgets, even from when we were so young she had no right to even ponder those happenings. She smiles coyly on the monitor.

"I recall a certain someone always fawning over his 'Viking' physique."

"Shh! The walls have ears around here."

"You're a newlywed, Atzi. Only a crazy person would put their ear to your door."

"There would be nothing to hear."

Wren blinks.

"What?"

"I said there would be nothing to talk about."

Wren does this weird thing with her face that looks like a cross between going cross-eyed and having just sucked on a lemon.

"You're kidding, right? You're married to Chike. Chike who always had a nude-y magazine hidden under his bed while we were in Shinka for the trials, and you're telling me there would be nothing for someone to hear?"

"He always had what?"

"Porn, Atzi! Pornography. He and Xipilli used to giggle about it during lunch like schoolgirls whispering about a cute boy. And you're saying that he didn't touch you once during your post-nuptial voyage?"

"Well, no. It's not that. We..." I trail off because I don't actually know what to call what we did. It doesn't feel right to say we made love. Nor would I call what we did sex, exactly. It was too mechanical for that. It also wasn't nearly exciting enough to merit any of the lewder terms for intercourse. Ah, there it is. "There was intercourse. Just on the first night. The rest of the time, he was a perfect gentleman."

"Gentlemen should at least provide their wives the most basic of pleasures during such a vulnerable time as their honeymoon."

"Wren, it's fine. I don't want to pressure him to—"

"Atzi?" I look up at the new voice entering the conversation.

"Chike! Sorry, I'm not dressed yet."

"No, I'm sorry. I should have told Maria I was on my way. I'll come back in a second."

He turns to leave.

"No, wait. You're alright. Let me just throw something on."

"No. I-I don't want to bother you."

"It's really fine, Chike. You don't have to."

"No, I really think—"

"*Hijo de la chingada!*" Wren's voice shouts over the monitor speakers. "You're not bothering her, *pendejo*. She wants to spend time with you. Just sit your ass down and wait."

Chike's cheeks, normally the color of brassy obsidian, warm to a ruddy purple.

"Alright, then. Since I have you and your sister's blessing, I suppose I will wait."

He looks so awkward standing there with his hands in his pocket, looking anywhere but at me as though he hasn't already seen me naked. Though, I suppose it was rather dark on our wedding night. I don't quite remember what he looks like under his clothing either.

I turn to the computer monitor.

"I'll talk to you later, sister."

Wren gives me her trademark twisting bunny ears wink and logs off.

I rise from the chair and give my husband a small curtsy.

"Your highness, if you'll give me a moment." As I pass through to my bedchamber, I call out. "What did you want to ask me about ... dear?" I don't know why I added that pet name. We've only been married a week. For all I know, he hates pet names. What if his mother used to call him that before she died? What if it reminds him of an ex-girlfriend who may or may not be an ex because of this arranged marriage thing? I decide to put it out of my mind as I make my way over to the folding screen where Maria normally lays out my dress for the day. However, I'm curious to find that, rather than the usual sundress or one of my more formal court outfits, she's laid out a casual pantsuit for me.

"Truth be told," comes Chike's voice from my sitting room, "I was hoping you'd be up for a bit of an adventure today."

"Adventure?"

The khaki outfit looks like one of those that you often see on vacation brochures for people wanting to take a tour through the Serengeti. A pressed button-down with a scarf tied around the woman's head and the type of trousers that look like they could handle a trek through the mud but would really just fall apart at the first true test of grit.

"You'll forgive the imposition, I hope, but I asked Maria to set out something more appropriate for a bit of a wilderness expedition."

"A wilderness expedition?"

Chike's face opens in the most enchanting of smiles.

MIDNIGHT CUMBIA

Ebele is very different from Deriva. It would have to be. It's part of the mainland, after all, but the climate is much drier, the people more weathered, the wildlife hardier.

I think Chike told me "orisumi" meant something along the lines of Sacred Refuge in the common tongue. The home of Ebele's royal family is beyond vast. The villa in and of itself is beautiful to behold, a rolling scape of chateaus and gazebos with a central pavilion where most festivities take place. Everywhere you turn, you can find carefully tended flowers, shaped hedges, and exquisite tapestries, and interlaced with all of that finery are the ancient statues and carved trees of the local tribes who first colonized this part of Ebele. What I love best, though, is the wildlife.

Orisumi borders over ten million acres of land, and the protected forest and savannah it sits in the heart of encompasses the entirety of the country—some 140 million acres. Twenty minutes into our so-called expedition and the villa has only just disappeared over the far end of the horizon.

"Chike, where are we going?"

He looks at me with a perfectly boyish grin. He really is a handsome boy. Only just beginning to grow out his facial hair, he really does look too young to be a technomancer. Never mind that he is on the older side for graduates.

"You'll see."

He clenches his tongue between his teeth, takes a firmer grip on the wheel, and accelerates. The hovercraft rushes forward so quickly, I have to slap my hat back onto my head before it too can take flight.

"Chike!"

His laughter is deep with just a touch of a dancing lilt at the end. It isn't loud and boisterous like his father's, just slightly more subdued. I could see him growing into such a laugh as the years progress, but I could also see his tone staying bright with the light of his youth through the years. It's the kind of laugh which can't help but remind me that he is two years younger than I am.

The scenery whizzes by. A rolling bustle of grasslands, savannah, and the occasional termite mound, and I can't get enough of the landscape. I wonder if Maria and I might come out here for a picnic at some point. I would love to photograph the landscape. Maybe at sunset? No, dawn would be better. I bet I could capture a breathtaking image of the sun rising up behind the trees.

"What is that?" I point to a large, seemingly upside-down tree in front of us.

"That's the great Baobab. It is the central marker of Orisumi. All of the land beyond this point is completely unchanged from when our ancestors first arrived in Ebele. As beautiful as it is, you should never come out here alone."

"Why not?"

"The Unseen Folk. As accommodating as they can be, the fae don't always take kindly to human+ on their reservation."

"We're going onto the reservation?!"

Chike's dark eyes twinkle.

As we were traveling to the villa from the docks where our yacht disembarked, I mentioned off-hand how it must be amazing seeing all of the animals on the grounds. Now, it would seem Chike has deemed it utterly necessary for me to experience those sights firsthand.

"I thought you said it was too dangerous to go on the reserve."

"Only if you're alone, my love. Only if you're alone..."

The second part of that statement goes unsaid, but I think I understand what he means, so I curl into his free arm and allow myself to enjoy the vision spreading out before me as my new husband introduces me to my new home.

And how wondrous a place I discover it is.

4

Wild Things

THE CHEETAH STALKS HER PREY FROM behind a nearby rock formation. She is alone and wholly dependent on her stealth in this endeavor. Should she fail, it will not only be she who goes hungry. Her kittens sit quietly in the grass behind her, learning so they too may become the hunter.

Her prey, a small herd of gazelles, ambles and grazes in the clearing beyond. The seven adults seem only about half aware of their calves romping and gallivanting around without a care in the world. Ah, to be as carefree as a newborn gazelle. I wish I could have such a worry-free existence.

But then the cheetah attacks.

The big cat launches itself toward the herd at what must be close to 100mph.

Chike passes me the binoculars, pointing me at the correct blur of spots.

"Watch her tail. That's how you'll know which direction she is going to go next."

I try my best, but my untrained and unaugmented eyes still can't keep up. The moment I find her, she curves herself in a new direction. By the time I find her next, the young gazelle is down.

"Incredible, isn't it?"

"It's unbelievable."

The victorious hunter makes a sound between a yip and a meow, and her kittens, three healthy young cheetahs, scamper up to the kill and dig in.

On the fringe of the clearing, not far from where the other gazelles have run away to, a lone cow (apparently that's what you call a female gazelle) stutters its hooves into the ground. There is something lost in the female gazelle's eyes. She stays for a moment as though hoping her eyes are deceiving her before she turns to return to the herd, calf-less.

It makes my heart hurt.

"The circle of life is indeed a cruel truth here on the savannah." My husband looks thoughtful as he speaks. "But it keeps our world spinning."

Chike and I set out on this adventure fairly early this morning. Now, it is nearing sunset.

In the hours we have spent on the reserve, I feel as if we have seen an entire planet. We've seen flocks of geese, a memory of elephants, an ostentation of peacocks, a cackle of hyenas, a pride of lions, and herds of mixed animals like zebras, antelope, and a family of giraffes. And those are just the animals we saw on the grassland plains. In the forests, there were skulks of foxes and a shrewdness of baboons. Chike stopped us in the lowlands and guided me down to the water where a bale of turtles were lounging on the edge of the water. Chike didn't want me to touch them, but I've handled sea turtles all my life. The only difference, apparently, is these will apparently take a good chunk out of your hand if you're not careful. Strangely enough though, I haven't seen any fae about. I can't help but think they are avoiding us.

This endeavor with the cheetah is only the most recent adventure we've witnessed. The sun rides low in the sky. In probably 30 minutes, it will touch the treetops, and in the hour following, it will likely touch the earth.

"The same is true of the ocean. The strong eat the weak, and when the strong cannot survive, it is usually indicative of a much bigger problem."

"Yes, the health of a land's predators often indicates the overall well-being of the ecosystem. It is largely the reason the Orisha established Orisumi some 75 years ago, not only as our home and hearth but also as a sanctuary for the wildlife of Ebele."

"What was happening before?"

Chike looks somber for a moment.

"Our predecessors were overzealous in their taming of the land. They hunted the local fauna to the brink of extinction and desolated the plant life. The rivers were so low the crocodiles couldn't submerge, so the antelope stomped on them. Five years of such neglect and abuse, and all of the river goddesses of Ebele rose in rage at the state of their children's suffering. They punished the peoples of the rivers and aired their grievances to the Orisha of the time."

I can't help but feel there's something in that statement which Chike is leaving unsaid. Technomancers did not used to be the super humans they are today. In fact, technomancers in their present hyper-augmented state have only really been around for the last hundred or so years. Ebele and Deriva did not have any such technomancers until roughly 50 to 75 years ago.

"By 'aired' you mean they killed them?"

Chike nods. "A whole generation of human+ wiped out at the whims of angry gods. The only ones left alive were the unaugmented. They gathered together and used the technologies which had been previously abused to found Orisumi."

"How did the people respond?"

"The general consensus was we needed to be more mindful of what kind of impact we have on the world around us. We shifted our usage of technology, traded might for nuance, and sought to merge with the natural world more than lay claim to it."

"So you chose to make the natural world better suited to a technolyzed world."

"In a word. We can't change human nature. That's what destroyed the hexen monarchies. They thought they could defeat progress, and in their attempts to fight it, they found themselves destroyed by innovation. Just look at Tanzita here." He gestures to the biomechanical elephant who has been our noble steed, a great beast of burden with augmentations in her lower limbs and a trunk reinforced with metal plating. There is more. I discovered after mounting her that her mechanical hind legs transform into monstrous wheels. "The hexen would have put her down after her accident. We saw more use in repairing the damage done. Now she is one of our most loyal beasts of burden and unspeakably more reliable than even the sturdiest vehicles of our neighboring nations."

Which explains the cyborgean modes of transportation in Ebele. I look down at the head of the biomechanical elephant currently acting as our mode of transportation. I thought it cruel at first that the Ebeleans used their technology to irrevocably alter the fauna under their care. I think I understand better now their goals behind such procedures. It is an act of mercy not of greed.

"Can I see the river apex?"

Chike looks at me, stunned. "You want to go into the lowlands?"

"Can we? I want to pay tribute to the goddesses who sleep in the soil of my new home."

"Okay." He adjusts himself in the saddle, taking hold of the reins. "Then let's go."

Tanzita rears up on her hind wheels, and in a burst of speed, we are away.

Wild Things

"Atzi," Chike calls.

It's dark now. The ride to the lowlands didn't take terribly long with Tanzita running at full speed. I know you wouldn't expect an elephant to be able to run very fast, considering the bulk of their size, but stampedes happen fast, and when an animal of such size and mass gives chase, you better believe you want to get out of the way as quickly as humanly possible. And that, mind you, is when considering unaugmented creatures.

"*¿Mande?*" I ask on instinct. "I mean, yes, what is it?"

"Are you sure you want to go down to the river?" Chike asks as he dismounts from his saddle around the elephant's neck. "It can be quite dangerous going near the water this soon after dusk. That's where the elokoi tend to lurk, and they are not to be trifled with."

"What's an elokoi?"

"May you never meet one is all I have to say. They are devilish little demons. They like to pretend to be sully fairies when really all they want is a pound of human flesh."

"How awful!"

"They are horrible little termites, for certain."

A part of me wants to still offer my sincerity to the river. Actually, a large part of me still wants to do so.

"Please, I just want to offer a prayer to the river before we go back. Maybe leave some of the wine from our picnic. You don't think something could happen all that quickly, do you?"

In the contrasting light of the moons and our lanterns, Chike's skin glimmers like oil. A part of me wonders off-handedly what it would be like to glide my fingertips over the sleek line of his biceps.

"Come on, Chike. Surely no elokoi is any match for you and Agni."

He sighs at my batting lashes.

"We will keep it quick," he says, his accent sliding into his speech as he holds his hand out to me. The thickness of the Ebelean tongue is so different from the lilting tonality of Derivan. The language is so fast-paced. I haven't been here very long, but I have heard Absko, Chike, and Chiamaka converse with one another enough to recognize it. Not to mention the speed with which the head butler of the household dictates assignments to the rest of his staff.

It is a little embarrassing, not being able to keep up. I can tell Chike is being mindful to slow his common speech down for my understanding.

I nod. "I understand."

I take his hand and allow him to help me from the elephant's back. In my free hand, I have a bottle of wine and a wrapped-up bundle of Derivan *pan dulce* tucked into my side.

He escorts me to the water's edge. I've never seen river water so still.

The waterways in Deriva are so voluminous. Always running, ever changing, they thunder down from the peaks of the mountains in torrents—thousands of horses racing to the sea.

This river moves slowly. So slowly in fact, I wouldn't even be able to tell it was moving were it not for the stray leaves and twigs floating down the steady stream.

The light of Chike's torch burns over the surface, highlighting the few stray glimmers of sleepy crocodilian eyes.

"They are waking for their evening meal."

"Will we be disturbing them?"

"Not so long as we avoid their preferred banks. The females often nest near the underbrush, and the males like to sun themselves on the beaches farther upstream. We should be fine in this area."

His words claim one thing, but his unbuckling of Agni tells another. He is on edge. I can tell he is on edge. It makes me feel foolish for insisting on coming down here, but if there was one thing my mother always instilled in me, it was to pay the proper respects to the gods wherever you may find yourself.

The water's edge is lined with lush grass and damp earth. I kneel, uncaring for the mud seeping into my pants.

I fold my body in half as I present the wine to the river.

"Para su familia, reina de la rio."

I open the bottle with a pop and pour the liquid into the water.

Next, I take the bread.

"Atzi es mi nombre. Yo soy de la Isla Deriva. May your heart be full and your love be great. *Mucho gusto."*

After I set the bread unwrapped at the river's edge, I press my lips to the earth: a *beso* hello and goodbye.

A frog croaks to my left then jumps into the water. For a moment, I can just barely make out the speck of light settled on its back—a fairy waving at me. I decide the little amphibian and its rider is acting as a messenger on my behalf, and as I make my way back to my husband, more than a few flickers of fairy light rise up out of the grass to light my footsteps.

Chike tells me later the name of such a fae is aziza.

The return home is filled with stories of Ebele, like how the hyena found its laugh or how the river learned to babble. Chike tells me stories of the gods and goddesses, of the creation myths which shaped the aboriginal fae who once ruled this part of the world before the witches came in as pilgrims to a land already claimed.

He speaks of a mother goddess, so old no existing tongue can truly speak her name, a warrior queen who smote the dark entities who kidnapped her children. She tracked them down and pulled their teeth from their skulls to make the stones of the earth. She used their skin to mold the great grassy plains and made the trees from their spines.

Maria waits for us at the top of the drive.

"Buenas noches, Señor y Señora."

"Buenas, Maria," I greet her in return. The woman bows unnecessarily. I've told her time and time again not to be so formal. This is the woman who bandaged my skinned knees and on more than one occasion allowed me to be sick all over her. She is so much more than a servant, but in her own words, *"En casa del herrero, cuchillo de palo."*

I couldn't tell you exactly what she meant by that proverb (The literal translation to comm goes something along the lines of "In the blacksmith's house, you'll find a wooden knife."), only that maybe she knew that she was expendable, never to profit from the work of her employers. In other words, the blacksmith only makes weapons for paying customers. The blacksmith's family does not pay; therefore, they use only a simple wooden knife. There are other turns of the same phrase: "The son of the shoemaker always goes barefoot" or "The seamstress's daughter only wears the rags." As hired help, she knows her place is not within the family, regardless of my fondness for her.

"Maria!" shouts Chike, addressing the woman with far more gusto than she is accustomed to. "The princess and I had a brilliant adventure, and I'd like to see her to her rooms personally. Why don't you take the evening to yourself? You've worked so hard to set up Atzi's rooms. You've earned it."

Maria looks from Chike to me, a blank expression on her face.

"Chike," I start quietly. "Maria does not understand common."

"Oh," he says, looking disheartened. "Well, I..."

"It's alright, darling. I'll translate for you."

I relay Chike's message to Maria, who seems more than a little miffed at being dismissed from her duties. In Deriva, there is no greater insult you can give to a working woman than to tell her to rest without accomplishing her duties.

"Está bien, Maria. Él no quiere hacer mal. Yo digo con el."

She is still somewhat miffed, but she curtsies to him and retires for the evening.

WILD THINGS

Several other handlers relieve Chike of Tanzita's reins. The poor bionic creature is running low on energy. The animal visibly sinks in relief as they plug her into the stable's power generator.

"My princess?"

Chike offers me his arm, and we walk together to my rooms.

Nerves jitter through my body. Is he going to spend the night? It wouldn't be unwelcome.

This is what it means to be married, isn't it? An opportunity to step down an unknown path and lay each stone as you go. I take a careful step into his space, not so close as to touch him, but I am definitely in his personal bubble. A goodnight kiss would not be unwanted nor inappropriate, all things considered. In fact, I think it would be a rather perfect way to end the evening.

My eyes slide shut, and I lean up onto my toes. But no kiss comes.

"Goodnight, princess."

My eyes snap open.

Chike bows his head to me and makes his way out of my rooms.

I've felt disappointment before. It's a commonplace emotion when Elisabeta De Claré is your mother: No's were fairly common growing up. No candy before dinner. No swimming after lunch. No playing in your temple clothing. *No, Atzi, you can't go and watch your siblings spar. You have your own lessons to see to, and I am not about to present a daughter to the public who is unable to articulate the meaning of our constitution to a fault.*

Disappointment is no stranger.

I, however, have never before felt it coupled with shame.

5

Mechanical Whir

A FEW DAYS FOLLOWING CHIKE'S LITTLE impromptu safari, Absko summons me.

"Princess Atzi, your majesty." The way the domo announces me is so formal. So contrary to the way Absko actually conducts his business. A boisterous laugh echoes from within his work room.

"Yes, of course. Let her in, man. Don't keep my daughter-in-law waiting!"

The domo looks entirely unimpressed when he opens the door to let me in. "Mademoiselle."

"Thank you, Abram."

"You're welcome, ma'am."

Absko's office reminds me of those old antique writing nooks many people spend thousands of credits to recreate nowadays. The floor-to-ceiling windows are dressed with parted draperies in the colors of Ebele, green and gold. His desk is a large, mahogany affair—hand-carved if the careful designs along the leg panels and table edges are to be judged accordingly. The walls are papered with a gorgeous pattern of vertical stripes interrupted by savannah grasses, florals, and fauna done in the most delicate of watercolor. Lions chase zebras along the panels while macaws fly around the room as brilliant as they might look in real life. At the lowest level, brazenly colored crocodiles and hippopotamuses swim through ripples of water.

If you were the kind to watch *peliculas* about royalty, you would see the directors often depict hunting trophies on the walls of the rich and powerful. If you were inclined to believe such portrayals, you might expect a man who is the king of the most wildlife-rich country in Deus to have at least some sort of taxidermized beasts on his wall.

There are none here. Not even a fish anchored to a plaque. Instead, there are tapestries of woven grass. There are planters of herbs and flowers. The walls are decorated with framed photographs of animals in the wild: a fox vixen taking care of her kits, a tiger bathing in the river, an eagle mid-dive with its talons extended for the helpless squirrel on the ground.

It's a beautiful room.

"Atzi, my darling!"

The Orisha greets me with a full outburst, arms held akimbo in greeting the way one welcomes a hug from a great friend.

"*Suegro,*" I greet him with a deep curtsy. Skin-deep, Absko looks quite young despite his years and experiences, wholly unbothered by his occupation. He is well groomed from the shine of his shaven head to the beads perfectly woven into the deep black hair of his long goatee.

"Never you mind those formalities. We are family now, remember." He embraces me in a hug that manages to warm me from my head to my toes. He is so much larger than my father, not taller but more built, and his augmentations make him even bigger, with the way his exoskeleton sits around his shoulders and chest. "Thank you for humoring this old king with a meeting. Are you settling in alright?"

I smile. "I'm doing well, *Suegro.*"

Mechanical Whir

"Excellent. Come, sit. We have much to discuss."

Papá once told Xipilli and me several stories about the various missions he and Absko used to go on in their youth. Mamá was present in a few of those, but they were mostly stories for the boys. From wrangling wild hogs to facing down whole howls of lycanthropes, there were quite a few stories that were hard to believe to begin with, and they only got more and more outrageous as they went on.

But the one that has always stuck with me is the story about how Absko's wife was killed by a witch. It was not too long after Chiamaka was born. There had been a threat on the outskirts of Orisumi. The local fae were terrorizing some of the villages, and Absko had called upon my papá to help him quell the cacophony. It should have been an easy mission, and for the most part, it was. Fae don't need much to be appeased, just a harmless sacrifice of food, drink, maybe some jewels and gold, and they then scamper away happy until the next time some human makes the mistake of wandering into their territory.

This wasn't that simple. It turned out later a witch had caused the ruckus to begin with, instigating the fairies into causing chaos so he could infiltrate the royal villa while the technomancers were away.

Suffice to say, by the time Absko and Tlanextli returned to the villa, the witch had come and gone, taking the young prince and princess with him. Absko's wife was left severely injured from trying to protect her children. From thence forth, the mission shifted from being a run-of-the-mill pest control objective to a life-or-death situation. Absko and Tlanextli wasted no time in rounding up the adepts in Orisumi to track down the witch. Obviously, we know Chike and Chiamaka were safely returned home, but the witch got away, and Absko's wife succumbed to her wounds.

He's been alone ever since. Just him and his two children. The whole story had been brought on after a seven-year-old

Xipilli mentioned something off-hand about how dumb this Orisha must be for the amount he smiles.

"He may seem boisterous and optimistic on the outside, Xipilli," our father had said. "But in reality, Absko is a man in pain. The way he deals with the loss is by making the world the best it can be in as far as he can control. It is why his people love him, why his son looks up to him so, and why he is his daughter's favorite playmate. You can learn a lot from a person like that. Perhaps, one day, when you are older and wiser, you might exemplify him and treat an unkind world with kindness rather than anger. Perhaps then you will change it for the better."

The lesson was meant for my more impetuous brother, I know, but I too took the lesson to heart. Absko is a tough man, to be sure. He wears his optimism and positivity like a shield against the horrors of the world we live in. Papá might carry the visible scars of a life in service to a war on the supernatural, but Absko carries the soul-deep weathering such an occupation might have beneath the skin.

"Chike was telling me all about your little endeavor on the reserve the other day. I hope you are finding our little corner of the world as enchanting as we do."

"It's amazing! All of the animals! It's unbelievable how rich the ecosystem is here. Besides marine life, we mostly only have monkeys, lemurs, and coatis in Deriva. I think the most dangerous land animal we have is a certain kind of tarantula. My sister used to call it the grandpa tarantula because it has what looks like a big old mustache on its back end."

I settle myself in the chair across from him behind the desk. As I sit, a rumbling sound greets me. From behind Absko's desk ambles a huge, biomechanical male lion. Chike told me that oftentimes, many of the technomancers of Ebele will take an injured animal, fix it up with augmentations, and then keep it as a battle companion. Chike himself has no such creature under his command, but he's only been a technomancer for a few months. This must be Absko's animal companion.

"Ah, Kwame. Have you decided to greet our Princess Atzi, yourself? She has come to us from very far away. Be kind, boy."

Absko's large hands are dwarfed by the size of this animal's head and mane. Big cats aren't supposed to be able to purr, but I could swear I hear some kind of rumbling sound happening in the great beast's chest.

Must be one of the augmentations.

Similar in construction to Tanzita, the lion has had its hind legs implanted with several pieces of tech. The forelegs have been replaced with spring-loaded canisters, probably to assist with bounding leaps and jumps. The lion's jawline too has been repaired with various mechanical joints and artificial teeth. I wonder if his jaw was broken by a trapper or a wild horse of sorts. I can also see the cabling that has been laid under his fur. It glows faintly in green lines of light. I wonder how much of the circuitry is meant to enhance what is already there and how much is there to provide necessary life-support for the creature.

"I thought Deriva was home to many a tropical big cat."

"Oh no. Jaguars and their like are more common in the Tai Tai. We have ocelots and servals sure, but they stay well away from any people, and the most damage they could do to even an unaugmented person could be mended with just a few stitches."

"Well, I'm glad to hear you find our home so unique. After all, it is your home now as well."

"Of course."

"As such, I thought it was time we discussed your augmentations."

I tilt my head in confusion.

"My augmentations, sir?"

"Yes, right now, you are only in possession of Derivan augmentations." He opens up a laptop to his left. "You already have the standard ID chip, your swim prosthetics, and your most recent cosmetic enhancements. Is all of that correct?"

"Yes, sir."

I'm not entirely sure why he is confirming like this. I already had to register all of my augmentations through the international transit services. Marrying into another country's royal family naturally requires even more paperwork than simply applying for a green card. Body scans, neural tests, and yes, even such archaic tests as a full blood work-up all need to be done before any marriage certificates can be issued to couples marrying from two different countries.

"I know. You're wondering why I am asking and checking all of these things, but the truth of the matter is all of your augmentations are Derivan in nature. On paper, you are the perfect example of a Moctezumo family member, yet you are now part of the Naga family. Should you not have Naga augmentations?"

"I'm not sure I follow, *Suegro*."

"How would you like to have one of the most foundational augmentations of the Ebelean royal family? Particularly for the women of the royal family."

"But I've only been here a week?"

"Yes, I realize this may be premature. Tradition dictates we wait until children are in the equation, but I find tradition superfluous at best. I've considered you a daughter ever since your parents and I agreed that you and Chike would make a perfect match."

I don't know what to say. I've never been very big on augmentations in general. I like the ones I have, and I think, as a concept, they can be very beneficial for those who need them, like my sister who is reliant on her prosthetic hand if she wants to properly use her aetherkalis. Mano is a perfect little handful on its own. I don't know who thought it would be a bright idea to allow the girl to tinker with her robotic limb, but tinker she did, and the damn thing is near sentient now. Even so, the only reason she has that artificial limb is because of the accident when we were younger. I doubt she would have opted to get such an augmentation were it not for that.

Not that there aren't plenty of people in the world who would choose otherwise.

I've heard of people willing to have limbs amputated solely for the purpose of getting the latest and greatest prosthesis on the market. Technolyzation, as they call it in places like Aighneas, Seraphim, and Murasaki. The practice is illegal in Deriva. I know it to not be so frowned upon in Ebele. However, to my knowledge, Chike and Absko have no such augmentations, and I doubt Chiamaka does either.

"What kind of augmentation are you referring to, my liege?"

"I am referring to our Auto Personality Simulators. It's a neural implant. It collects data on your personality over time with the purpose of creating a virtual replica of you."

"A virtual replica?"

"Of sorts. It would take time to develop of course. It takes up to four or five years before the chip gathers enough data to be indistinguishable from the real thing, but in the event of an emergency, it could allow you to broadcast yourself into another location for security purposes."

Well, that certainly seems interesting, and maybe somewhat sinister. "Everyone in Ebele has this?"

"Only the royal family. Chike and Chiamaka have had their APS implants since they were babies. I would hope my grandchildren would also have the implant, but I will leave that for you and Chike to discuss."

I don't know how I feel about putting a neural implant in a baby. In Deriva, mechanical enhances are only given to children in the wake of an accident or otherwise existing necessity. Even in Murasaki, children need to be a certain age before they can receive their S33d.

"I don't know, but thank you, Majesty."

"Well, give it a thought, and let me know. I would hate for my daughter-in-law to be left vulnerable in the event of a national crisis, but if you don't want it, then you don't need it."

6

Gossip Girl

THE CABIN ROCKS GENTLY SIDE TO SIDE. It's a good night for sailing. A good night for a honeymoon. I sit demurely at the edge of the bed. Maria has taken away my wedding gown. I am now dressed for my first night alone with my new husband.

I wring my hands. Mamá used to always get upset with me for this one nervous tic I have, but I can't help it. There is nothing else I can do as I wait anxiously for my husband to come out of the bathroom. He has been in there for a while. I wonder if he is as nervous as I am.

"Maria," I call.

"Sí, Señora."

"¿Me haces una taza de té, por favor?"

"Se como quiere, Señora."

"Si, por favor."

Maria turns to go to the galley.

"Wait! Esperame."

I race to my bags and pull out the beautiful container of tea leaves my sister gifted to me right before we boarded the boat.

"Una taza de eso. Please, I want this one."

She looks at me, confused for a moment. She knows I much prefer a very bland citrus green tea. The leaves Wren has arranged for me are far more complex: rose hips and orange peel with a bitter red tea leaf. There are other things in there, too. I just don't remember everything Wren listed when she was telling me the concoction's contents. But, despite her confusion, Maria takes the jar and leaves.

Ten minutes later, she returns with a steaming cup of tea. Chike, however, is still in the bathroom.

A few weeks later, Wren comes to visit.

"*Princesa?*"

"*Sí, Maria?*"

I'm out on the verandah reading a book on Ebelean politics. I figure I should educate myself on how things have historically been done in my new home since I am now married to the man who shall be the next Orisha of this country. Not only that, but by extension, since Chike's father as yet remains unmarried, I am the highest ranking female in Ebele.

"*Su hermana está aquí.*"

I snap my book shut and hop up onto my feet. Wren didn't tell me anything about stopping in for a visit on our last video call.

"Wren is here?"

"*Sí, Señora. Quería sorprenderle con una visita.*"

"*Tráela.*"

Maria disappears, and a plain moment later, my dark-haired, bright-eyed little sister comes racing around the corner.

"Atzi, darling! *Tu m'as manqué!*"

Wren, as always, brings *chisme*. We gossip the way you would expect any teenage girls to gossip. There's a reason

Xipilli always called us *chismosas*. Apparently, Papá is having a time with Xipilli's hotheaded readiness for action. Mamá broke another training room. One of the servant girls is sneaking out to see a boy. The same boy, apparently, is making advances toward Xipilli. And most interestingly enough, our dear, ever-annoyed brother appears to have developed a crush on the newly graduated technomancer Papá signed onto Deriva's roster, a young lady by the name of Irene.

I take my turn to speak, of course, telling Wren all about the various trips onto the reserve Chike has taken me on. We've gone out three times since the first instance Chike loaded me onto Tanzita and set us out for a picnic in the wilds.

"I mean it, Wren. You would not believe how incredible it is here. We have got to have Chike show you around the savannah. I feel like every time we go out, there is something new to see. You've just got to experience it."

My sister looks different since I last spoke to her.

"I'm glad you are doing well, sister."

Something in her eyes is off. It's the same look she gets after a blow out with my mother. For all that I love my mother, I am not blinded by my affection for her. Elisabeta has always been distant, if not outright cruel to Wren. It got worse after Freya died in more ways than one: having her undergo Firefly training on top of her adept/technomancer training, not allowing her to properly study without having an excessive number of chores and/or duties finished prior, never allowing her to attend court with Xipilli and I, lest she was in the back of the room and acting as the hired help. I always hated it when my mother bullied Wren simply for existing, whether she realized her behavior was abusive in nature or not.

"*Tough love, my darling,*" my mother called it. "*Wren is not a princess or a Moctezumo; she is, therefore, not guaranteed the same gifts and distinctions as you and your brother. She needs to learn hardship, lest she be unable to take care of herself once she leaves this cushy nest her father has made for her.*"

"Is it my mother?"

Wren blinks. *"Que?"*

"What did she do this time? I know she can be a right terror toward you. What is wrong? Something is wrong. I can tell."

"Nothing is wrong, Atzi."

"Don't lie to your big sister, Wren. You can never fool me. I know you too well."

Instead of sighing, which would be far more lady-like, Wren blows an outright raspberry.

"It's not your mother."

"Wren," I draw out the vowel in her name long enough to let her know I don't believe her for a moment.

"It's not your mother," she insists. "It's..." She trails off in a very un-Wren-like way.

"What is it?"

She huffs. "You can't tell anyone about this."

Whoa! That was not only a little abrasive but also surprising.

"Wren, who am I going to tell around here? Chiamaka much prefers paying attention to her gossip column than me, Maria, even if I did tell her, can't actually speak with anyone else around here, and I sure as hell am not going to tell Chike one of my sister's secrets."

Wren gives me a long look.

"Atzi."

"Okay, yes. I will say it. *En el nombre de Dios*, I will not tell anyone any words which are about to pass between us."

"*Bueno*..." Wren relaxes just a little bit. Anxious as I am to hear the *chisme*, I don't want to push for her to tell me. Clearly whatever this is weighs heavy on her. She'll talk when she's ready.

Maria came out not long after Wren's arrival to bring us some tea and crumpets. Wren made a face at the taste of the yerba mate that is so popular here and now sits scowling into the tea cup as if it had personally wronged her. She takes after

Papá, much preferring her coffee to anything else, though she is not terribly opposed to a black or green tea. I suppose that might be because those teas are a little stronger than others. When we were kids, Wren once took a sip of her mother's bedtime herbal tea. She promptly made a face, spat it out, and said it smelled like watered down plants. Herbal teas are the popular drink here in Ebele. We probably could find coffee for her somewhere on the grounds, but it won't be readily available in the kitchens, considering none of the royal family drinks it, and to my knowledge, none of the staff does either.

As I am nearly done with my own cup, Wren speaks.

"I slept with Kaito."

And I promptly spit out my tea, choking and sputtering so badly I can't breathe. My sister hurries around to pat my back through the coughing fit. When my airway clears, I notice her dabbing the tail of my *trenza* with a napkin. Ugh, I spit tea into my hair.

"You—you what?!"

"I. Slept. With. Kaito."

"Kaito, as in Kaito Miyazaki. Prince—in your own words—'stick-up-his-culo' Kaito Miyazaki?!"

"The very same."

"Wren!"

"What?"

"I thought you hated him!"

"I did. Well, okay, no I didn't. Not really. He was fun to tease is all."

"But you told me he hated your guts."

"Yeah, that's the part I'm still mildly confused about, but if his words are to be believed, he actually said he admired me."

"So, wait, wait, wait. When did this happen? When did you even see him?"

"You remember that Lorelei mission."

"But I thought four of you went."

"We did. We decided to split up in pairs to cover more ground. Xipilli went with Hikaru, and I went with Kaito. Long story short, Kaito and I ended up trapped in the catacombs—"

"The catacombs? The catacombs! Wren, you lost your virginity in a graveyard?!"

"So?" She seems taken aback by my outburst.

"Wren!"

"What? It's just dirt. Better than losing it on a dirty warehouse mattress because your partner was too cheap to buy a hotel room and couldn't risk having their parents catch the two of you."

I blink three times. What a strangely specific example, but Wren moves on. "Anyway, as I was saying, we were stuck under the city after a close encounter with the witch responsible for all of the disappearances. A real piece of work, by the way, but I'll spare you the details. We were waiting down there for a while, and I guess one thing led to another and well..."

"Well, how was it?"

Wren's cheeks go cherry red.

"It was kind of nice actually."

"Wren," I growl.

"What! Do you want a play-by-play or something?"

"Well, no, but..." I say, feeling more than a little miffed. She's being vague on purpose, and I do not appreciate it. I've never been one to entertain the green-eyed demon, but how is it my unmarried sister is getting more ... more ... (I don't want to say more sex. That's just so terribly lewd) more affection and intimacy when my husband lives just a compound away? I need something, damn it! Chike, for all the sweet dates he takes me on, refuses to even so much as kiss me goodnight. "You can't blame me for being curious. It's not like I have anything notable to compare to."

I don't quite realize what I just said until I finish watching the veritable array of thoughts and emotions pass over my little sister's face. First, the indignation fades away. Said indignation is replaced by exasperation, but then confusion crosses her face. A giant question mark may as well be holo-projected over her head. Lastly, shock (or maybe horror) opens up her features.

"I mean. Wait, no. I don't mean it like that."

"You mean your husband has been neglecting his duties. It's been nearly a month, and my sister hasn't gotten any action since that pathetic performance on her wedding night."

Wren stands, and my heart just about leaps out of my chest when she makes a beeline for the other end of the compound.

"Wren, where are you going?"

"To give that man a piece of my mind. No one rejects my sister and gets away with it, especially her own stupid husband."

The shoes I'm wearing are not conducive to running down the hall after my very much augmented technomancer of a sister. I didn't realize exactly how much more efficient those advanced/specialized augmentations would be. Christ, she seems almost as fast as the jackals Chike and I saw on the trail yesterday.

"Wren, please. You don't even understand what I was saying."

"Am I wrong?"

No...

"Well, maybe he's just shy!" I answer instead.

"Shy, my ass! No one gets to make my sister feel undesirable!"

Mind you, she shouts this just as we are passing some of the villa's staff.

"Wren!"

I sprint forward as fast as I can and try to grab her by the collar. She dodges, of course, but I manage to catch her by the elbow.

"Wren, it really doesn't matter if he wants me or not because I'm pregnant!"

The technomancer stops herself so fast, she nearly wipes out all over the tile.

"You're what?"

"I'm—" I nearly shout it aloud again as a pair of guards trek by, so I lower my voice to a hush. "I'm pregnant, and I really would rather my baby have a father by the time they arrive."

Wren looks at me, pale as a ghost and twice as silent.

"What?"

She thrusts her chin forward to something behind me. When I turn around, Chike is standing there, frozen stiffer than a turkey the week before Thanksgiving.

7

Fuego

*"Why should anybody read a fairy tale when there's a
pixie next door and a gnome in the garden?"*
A quote from *Book of Wings and Dust*
by Mothram Gryme, a hexen folklorist and hadologist

Orisumi – 31st Day in the Month of Fire

I'M DREAMING. I MUST BE.

"Have you ever seen how quickly things can go south?"

There is a strange, sugary-sweet smell in the air. My feet
are cold, bare as they are against the wood paneling of the
villa's central walkway. Why am I barefoot? I never walk outside barefoot. Not since Chike warned me against all of the
ants and termites that like to dwell in the long grass.

A shiver runs down my spine.

"Who are you?" My voice quivers on the air. "Where
are you?"

"My name is Aziza. I wanted to talk to you."

Aziza... As in those little fairies Chike and I found nesting near the river the other day. That's what they were called right?

"Are you a fairy?"

"Of sorts."

"Why are you talking to me?"

The fae giggles.

"I thought you were pretty, so I wanted to talk to you."

"If you wanted to talk to me, wouldn't it be more polite for you to reveal yourself to me?"

"As you wish, your highness. Hold out your hand."

A shimmer passes over my vision, and with a small puff of air, a tiny fairy perches on my thumb. No bigger than my pinky, the fairy has a lovely lavender complexion, like sand at dawn when the sun is just starting to peek over the hilltops, complete with bright red hair and wings to match.

"You're so pretty."

"Thank you, your highness. Do you like my wings?"

The little fae spins around on the top of my hand. The initial red I saw is not nearly the beginning or the end of the fairy's colors. The wings themselves are a kaleidoscope of color. It reminds me somewhat of a monarch butterfly's patterning but with the shaping of a luna moth and twice as luminescent.

"They are very lovely."

The fairy laughs. "You know. You're alright. I was worried about you because you seemed sad. If you ever need anything, give me a call. Just call my name three times."

"What is your name?"

"Aziza. What's yours?"

"Atzi."

"Atzi...?"

"Nagi. Atzi Nagi."

"What a beautiful name."

The statement echoes in my head until dawn calls me from my slumber.

FUEGO

When I wake up, Wren is looking at me with worry from the far side of the bed. "You okay, Atzi?"

"Yeah," I whisper. "Just a weird dream."

"What about?"

"Oh, nothing. Probably just a result of that strange dish we ate last night."

I don't want to worry her. She's leaving today for a mission, and the last thing I want to do is have her stressing about some silly dream.

"Oh, yeah, I had some weirdness from that too. What was it called again? Gorgnetal meat. Why don't they just call them what they are? *Escargot en flambe.* I thought I was going to burn my tastebuds off eating that."

"I thought you liked it."

"Oh, I did. I just didn't appreciate having to sit on the toilet for thirty minutes afterward."

"Wren!"

"Atzi!" she mocks back at me, flinging off the covers to get up. She moves about the room, gathering her stuff and packing up her travel bags. It's been nice having her here for the last couple of days. After the bomb drop in front of Chike that nearly resulted in my husband's untimely demise, Chike has steered clear of the two of us. I don't know if he is angry with me for not telling him first or if he is afraid of Wren.

I heard plenty of funny stories in regard to the boys' antics in relation to my sister at the trials. From the way Xipilli tells said stories, Wren gave them all the runaround. From the way Wren tells them, you would think they were barely passing meetings that started and ended at "hello, goodbye." From the way Chike tells them—and I'm more inclined to believe Chike than either one of my siblings—Wren left those boys with at least a few broken bones.

Actually, now I think on it, it probably was Wren who kept him away. Especially considering my little secret came out while she was on a tirade for the man's blood based on the simple notion that he hadn't fulfilled his "husbandly duties."

So, whether he's angry or scared, I don't really care. Either way, it's been a nice reprieve from having to deal with that loaded weapon.

"Are you sure you don't want to stay an extra day? It is your birthday tomorrow, after all."

"Yeah, I need the travel time. Something or someone is causing trouble along the Murasaki coastline, and they need a Derivan technomancer to check it out. I'm all for underwater dives and stuff, but they better give me a warm wetsuit. Temp regulators or no, those waters are freezing even at the peak of summer."

"Well," I lament, reaching under my bed for the gift I wrapped for her, "you should wear this on your trip."

"Atzi, you didn't have to."

"Of course, I did. You're my only sister, after all. Happy early birthday, Wren."

She opens the wrapping paper to find the gold arm cuff I had made for her. It's a musical staff with the notes to one of Wren's favorite songs written into it.

"It's so pretty!"

Something odd twangs in my gut at the word "pretty." I can't be sure why. Something recent I should probably remember but can't for the life of me figure it out. *Me olvidé.*

"You're leaving after breakfast, right?"

"I think so."

"Well, let me call Maria," I say, wrapping my house coat around my shoulders. "I bet she would be happy to make you some of her famous French toast."

"Ladies," a hesitant voice calls from the doorway. It's far too early for any of the wait staff to be knocking. I look over to find Tsun Lee, Chike's valet, peeking in.

"Ah, Tsun Lee, what brings you all the way to this side of the compound?"

"Yes, ma'am. His highness was wondering if the Lady Wren might like an escort to the river whenever she is prepared to leave."

"You mean he sent you all the way over here because he was too afraid to show his face after all this time? Couldn't he have sent a comm message?"

"Wren, please."

She crosses her arms with a huff.

"His highness finds comms to be impersonal. As to why he did not come in person, I do not know, my lady, but you can ride Tanzita and make it there in half the time."

Wren looks at me for an answer. I just shrug my shoulders at her.

"If Prince Chike's day is not too full, I would be happy to have him as an escort. Though I advise you to tell him to bring Agni, just in case."

"Of course, my lady. I will let him know. Additionally, *princesa*, his royal highness is wondering if he could join you for lunch upon his return."

My appetite dries up.

"Of course, Tsun Lee," I say. "He is welcome anytime."

"When were you going to tell me?"

As promised, Chike joins me for lunch after escorting Wren to the river docks where her skimmer is docked. I'm pleased to find my husband mostly unharmed, if a little pensive, in the wake of my sister's departure. I can't help but be curious about what may or may not have been said during the hour's trip to the riverside they took together. I'm sure Wren gnawed his ear off, but it really isn't my business to ask.

Chike's question is not said in a rude way or anything. In fact, we've been having a rather pleasant conversation about a certain breed of wolf that lives in the area along with the possibility of a late evening walk to the pond later.

I fold my napkin carefully into my lap before answering.

"I have a doctor's appointment scheduled for tomorrow. I was going to let you know once I knew for certain."

"We've only been intimate the one time."

I nod.

"Well, they certainly didn't lie to us in biology class. All it takes is one time."

"I was hoping we would have more time."

"What do you mean?"

"We can't call this off if there is a baby."

I can't believe what I'm hearing. "Call this off?"

"We can't divorce if you're pregnant. It would be a shame on you and on me."

"You want a divorce."

"I mean isn't it better to have the option?"

My stomach drops into my feet.

When I was eight years old, my mother threw a plate across the table at my father. I don't remember why, exactly, she decided to throw the dinnerware at his head, but I do remember how livid she was.

It was the largest outburst I have ever seen from my mamá before or since, and this was after years of marriage to my father. I must really be my mother's daughter if my fingers are itching to throw the water glass straight into his face.

But, you know, when I think about it, would that be such a bad thing?

"Atzi?" I've been quiet for too long apparently.

I take the glass, I take a sip, and without any fanfare, I throw the whole thing straight in his face.

"Atzi!"

Chike stumbles to his feet, taking half of the table with him while I simply get up, signal for Maria to grab my coat, and head for my rooms.

Chike, however, isn't smart enough to leave me be.

"What in the hell was that for, woman?! Are you crazy?"

Woman! He dares to call me "woman"!

"'What was that for?'" I parrot back to him. "'What was that for?' My husband of one month all but tells me he wants a divorce, yet I'm the crazy one!"

I turn back on my heel and storm away. I don't care what he has to say. I don't care if he even has anything to say. How dare he? How dare he!

"Atzi, wait. That's not what I meant."

"Save it!"

"Atzi, please."

"If you didn't want to marry me so badly, why didn't you say something to the people who decided to marry us in the first place? Then we wouldn't be in this mess to begin with, and you could go chase as many skirts as you wanted, just like you did during the trials."

"Atzi, no. That's not what I meant."

"I don't care what you meant."

"Atzi! I'm sorry," he shouts, catching my upper arm before I can slam the door in his face. "Will you let me explain, damn it? It came out wrong, and you've misunderstood."

I stop walking for fear of having my arm ripped off by a superhuman.

"Explain to me how I've misunderstood. You barely touched me on our wedding night. You'll barely even hold my hand when we go out on the reserve. Goddess forbid you so much as kiss me. Meanwhile I'm over here nervous I'm doing something wrong because my husband is not doing what I was told all husbands would do, which is share my bed and share intimacy with me. Now, with everything decidedly not happening, how could you saying you wanted to keep our options open for divorce mean anything other than you want a divorce?"

Chike's eyes look frantic as he studies my face.

"I don't want a divorce, okay? That wasn't what I meant."

"Well, then what the hell did you mean?"

"I wanted to take things slowly with you, Atzi. Treat you right, show you my world, let you decide whether you want to be married to me at all, but with a baby in the mix... Well, there's nothing we can do but make do with the situation."

Oh, gods above, my face is getting hotter. My vision is blurring. I'm about to cry. All the signs are there. I don't even know why.

"Do you not want to be married to me?"

Chike's expression softens. His eyes, previously wide with panic, relax. He's quite the picture with his shirt soaked through with the water I threw at him. Did he have to wear a white shirt today? I can see every line, every crevice, every outline of every muscle on that toned torso. It's not fair. He shouldn't be allowed to look so good while I just know my face would be blotching were it not for my cosmetic augmentations. The water dews in his hair.

"Atzi..."

"What?"

He smiles.

I have never wanted to slap a smiling person across the face like I want to now, but just as I'm about to raise my hand and swing, my *pinche vato* of a husband leans in. He wraps his arms around my shoulders, tugs me into him—wet shirt and all—and brings his lips to mine. It's the first kiss we've shared in a month.

La Rumba Encanto

CHIKE MAY BE YOUNG, BUT HIS BODY is that of a warrior.

When we were little, Xipilli developed this asinine obsession with an old-world sport called football. Teams of men would wear strange suits of armor and collide together in combat over an egg-shaped "ball." I couldn't make any sense of it beyond this point. Why would you call something that isn't shaped like a ball a "ball"? Balls are supposed to be spherical, an even radius on all sides with a perfect rotational axis. That is the definition of the thing. The so-called "ball" these football players passed around was decidedly not ball-shaped. It was elliptical and more torpedo-like in its usage. It didn't bounce very well; in fact, in this sport, if the football—I have another problem with this nomenclature because the ball is only kicked a few times a game—hit the floor, it was considered an end to the play. The ball also wasn't designed to be hit by anything. They just tossed it from player to player...

But I digress, we're talking about Xipilli's obsession after all, not my problems with said obsession.

Midnight Cumbia

My little brother started collecting these playing cards of old football players.

On the cards were representations of many of the players from the time period, some span of five years between 1945 and 1950 A.D., all of them wearing these plain jerseys with seemingly arbitrary numbers on them. At the bottom of the cards were stats for each player: number of field goals, successful passes, touchdowns, etc. I remember thinking it strange all of the players were so pale. I don't know if that's because there were no dark-skinned people in the old world or if there were problems within the various cultures that prohibited them from playing, but all of them were built to take some pretty impactful hits.

All this to say that in the old world, people may have said my husband was built like a football player, but the description falls short by our standards here in Deus.

Fine pectorals cushioned by washboard abdominals, there is strength in his torso. There would have to be, considering the weapon he wields. Agni is no handgun, that's for certain. And yet, I am still awed by his ability to lift me so easily. His arms are nearly as thick as the boiúna he wrestled the day we went safari riding through Orisumi's rolling grasslands. I thought he was just doing it to show off, and he was, if we are being honest. What hot-blooded male technomancer wouldn't take the opportunity to slay a netherbeast in front of their new wife simply for the sake of killing a netherbeast? Two birds with one laser beam as it were. But I found out the other day, said boiúna had attacked one of the children in the nearby village. Chike's showmanship had been a ruse for actually handling a problem which could very well have resulted in the deaths of who knows how many people in a short span of time.

Now, those muscles used to wrestle a highly deadly snake into submission envelop me in the best comfort I could ask for. When Chike pulls away, I don't know what to think. I don't know what to do. All I know is I really don't want him to go away.

"Atzi... Atzi... Atzi, darling, you've got to talk to me. Did I just—fuck! I fucked up, didn't I?"

He waffles in place.

"No, Chike—"

"Alright, you've got to hit me. I promised your sister I would let you hit me if I ever overstepped my rights, and Atzi, if I've overstepped in any way, I need you to hit right now."

He doesn't hear me. My voice is too small, and he's too busy having a veritable panic attack over a little kiss.

"My father is going to kill me. I promised him I would do my best to make you happy, yet here I am making a muck of it—"

I grab him. "Chike!"

He stops and stares at me. "Yes, my love?"

Now his full attention zeros in on my face, and my cheeks burn. "You don't have to panic. I did like it. I just didn't know what to say and I'm, well... I'm shy, okay?"

It seems to take him a moment to register my words. When he does, a goofy grin splits the technomancer's face.

"Wait, so then can I do it again?"

This time, I do actually slap him. Not hard. I wouldn't want to break my own hand on a technomancer's reinforced biology. But the tap is sharp enough to give the man a nice, somewhat playful warning.

And it certainly works, if the arousal sparking in Chike's dark eyes is anything to go by.

"This is why I've had a crush on you since I was twelve years old."

"Chike, if you like being beaten up, the better choice would have been my sister." Though she seems to be spoken for these days.

"No, not because you just hit. I've always liked you because you're sweet and gentle, yet you don't put up with your siblings' bullshit. Xipilli is a little turd, but when you're around, he shuts up and actually makes smart decisions."

"Does he now?"

"For sure! You're an amazing person, you know that?"

"Mhmm... So are you going to continue gushing about me, or are you going to make up for neglecting your duties as a husband this last month?"

The boyish smile quirks up into a smirk, and before I can even register any movement, my lips are once again claimed. Chike's grassy musk envelops me like a warm blanket. He smells like sun-warmed earth and morning dew. His hands rest at my hips. His pulse beats into my breast, and when I shift my body weight further into his, something else pulses against my lower belly.

"My prince. It would seem as though your body has run away with you."

"If you'd like, I can make yours run away, too."

I smile up at him through my lashes.

"That sounds tempting."

"Does it now?"

I nod. In the next moment, my feet are swept out from under me. My laughter rings out through the courtyard, and before I can even wonder where we are planning to go, Chike has already set off in the direction of my rooms. It feels like I blink, and my door is closing behind us. Just Chike and I alone at last.

For the next handful of days, Chike and I remain seemingly joined at the hip, if not closer in the nights. We spend the day on the grounds, watching the animals and helping the local villages with various tasks. Chike helps me weave baskets for the village households while Maria helps me jar various jellies and pick medicinal herbs from the villa's gardens for the townsfolk.

Chike accompanies me on my scheduled appointment to the doctor. He holds my hand as the doctor confirms that, yes, we are expecting. As we speak, Chike's first heir is growing in my belly. Healthy, with a strong heartbeat and every opportunity for growth.

When we arrive back home, Chike is so enamored by the idea of my pregnancy he spends what must be at least an hour worshiping my belly, waist, and my most secret places later that evening.

This is what I was expecting when we set out for our honeymoon voyage to Ebele. Eating, drinking, and exploring together, exploring each other between the soft silk of the sheets, learning what it means to be husband and wife.

I'm not bitter that it took us a month to have a true honeymoon. I just wish Chike would have clued me in to what his plans were. Looking back on it, it's kind of sweet he wanted to take things slowly. He didn't have to. Most men given a new young wife would be happy to perform and ask for said nightly duties as often as could be obtained. I've heard some pretty disgusting quotes about marriage, most of them directed toward women.

"A good wife is one who serves her husband in the morning like a mother does, loves him in the day like a sister does, and pleases him like a prostitute in the night."

"What we love about love is the fever, which marriage puts to bed and cures."

"A good marriage would be between a blind wife and a deaf husband."

I can't say any of those sayings are the most comforting, and I'm too young in my newly found connection to my husband to confirm or deny such axioms, but I do hope we can stay just like this for a while longer, learning and loving each other step by step as we navigate "us."

Chike has taken to sleeping in my chambers. It makes more sense. My rooms are bigger. Designed for a not-so-far-away future where I'll be taking care of our children, my place in the villa is basically a small house. Chike's rooms are more like a dormitory: a small bedroom and a work/meeting space should he need it. As a technomancer, though, he is not expected to be in-house as much as the rest of the family.

A few days after that fateful toss of water, the dawn greets us through the wooden blinds of my windows.

My body is bare, hidden only by a thin sheet. Chike too is naked, the impressive expanse of his torso exposed to my eye, a delicious sight. Who needs breakfast when such a feast is laid out before me? So naturally, I lean forward and take a bite.

Chike snorts awake at the nip to his ribcage. "Atzi. You know I'm ticklish there."

"Good morning, my love. You should wake up. Today is the meeting your father was telling us about at dinner. Remember he said it was important."

He grunts and snakes an arm around my hips, rolling me into him. He's trying to get me underneath him again, but I dodge his movements and worm my way up to straddle his hips.

"Now, none of that, sir. You are needed in the communication room."

"I don't want to go."

I plant a kiss on his chin. He angles his head, trying to deepen the kiss, but I duck away. He doesn't like this, vocalizing his point of view with a tortured groan. "Atzi," he whines.

"Chike," I whine right back to him. "What if I went with you?"

"Why would you want to sit in on a boring diplomatic meeting?"

"Because you're there."

"Right, and I'm sure it has nothing to do with being able to say 'hi' to your mom and pop."

"And Xipilli, too, of course, but I can call them anytime. How often do I have the chance to support my husband in his first big meeting as a fully ordained technomancer?"

"Is this really the first one?"

"It is, my love. You only graduated six months ago. This is the first convening of nations since the trials."

I roll myself off of him and the bed. I snatch a pair of his trousers off the floor and throw them in his face.

"Come on. I shan't be kept waiting, my prince."

"Oh, I'm so going to make you regret this later."

"I look forward to it, prince. Now get up!"

9

Thunderstruck

THERE ARE A LOT MORE PEOPLE IN THE throne room than I was expecting. Chiamaka and Absko, I expected. I wasn't expecting the various other technomancers on Ebele's roster to be present. Naturally, with those technomancers come the bionic beasts that characterize technomancy in Ebele. Biomechanical animals of all shapes and sizes: one man has a hyena at his side, another a jackal, a pair of women seem to share between them a small clowder of serval cats, and one particularly large man sits astride a large wildebeest.

Between the animals and the people, there's a lot of tech in the room, and it is lethal.

It's somewhat overwhelming.

Chike seems to sense my unease, so he reaches for my hand. People are looking at us. This is how I realize this is our first public presentation as husband and wife, a truth which is particularly driven home when Absko's majordomo announces our entrance as "Their Royal Highnesses, Prince Chike Nagi and his Princesa Atzi Nagi nee Moctezumo."

The throne room at Orisumi is a sight to behold.

The length of an indoor arena or gymnasium, the space easily hosts the vast amount of people currently gathered, but this is not the impressive part. The throne itself, where Absko currently presides, sits on a raised stone pillar. Across from him, at the center of the floor plan, a great iroko tree rises into the very top of the room. The tree by itself is impressive for its mass with a trunk the diameter of at least five grown men and a body of leaves more luscious than anything I have ever seen in Ebele. But it is not the organic parts that make this a landmark structure to beheld.

It is the inorganic parts.

Cables and wires circle through, in, and around the mighty body of the tree. Green lights glow with synthetic life along its branches. A super computer, powered by the tree itself, lives in the heart of this tree. Its monitors sit, nested in the branches about large enough for all present to get a perfect view of the happenings on screen.

The Aighnean president, the empress of Murasaki no Yama, and the pharaoh of Seraphim are each displayed on their own monitor. The screen where Papá should appear is currently awaiting connection. Odd. Papá is always on time for these kinds of events.

"Never make anyone wait on you, Atzi," he once said to me. "The petty have long memories, and the honorable do not deserve to be kept waiting."

It's still roughly five more minutes before the meeting is scheduled to begin. Maybe they are having connection troubles in Deriva.

"Chike, Atzi, come join me up here."

Absko gestures to the other set up of seats on either side of him. Chiamaka already sits in one of the smaller thrones, but there are two more set up on either side of the Orisha and waiting for us, the heirs to Ebele's spiritual monarchy.

Chike escorts me to my seat on Absko's left. As I settle in, Absko leans over. "It has been a while since I last spoke to your father. I'm sure you are looking forward to seeing your family."

"Of course, *Suegro*. The only one I've really spoken to is Wren."

"Ah, yes, she came to visit, did she not?"

"Yes, sir."

"Just like your sister, dropping in unannounced. She really is a free spirit."

"That's Wren. She goes where her whims take her, and a prayer for anything or anyone who might get in her way."

The minutes tick by, and still Deriva's monitor stays blank until Tlanextli is officially late.

"It is time to begin. Should we proceed without him?" asks President Gewalt, obviously referring to my father.

"I've never known Tlanextli to be tardy to an important meeting," says Empress Mirai.

"I spoke to Tlanextli not three days ago. He said he was looking forward to this conference. That he is late is rather odd and disappointing. Princess Atzi had been so looking forward to seeing her family."

"Let us hope it is not an urgent matter that keeps him," inserts the pharaoh.

"Indeed."

The proceedings begin with several of the leaders recounting concerning instances with Seraphim: border disputes, ghouls in their mainframes, and other asunder mishaps that look more and more suspicious. I don't pay it any mind though. I'm too busy messaging my family.

[Xipilli, what is papá doing? Did he get the time zone wrong again? The meeting has started.]

[Papá, is something wrong with your comm systems? Everyone has started without you.]

[Mamá, what is papá doing?]

[Wren, are you home? Papá is supposed to be in an important meeting, but he's late. He's never late.]

None of them answer me.

"Atzi, are you okay?" asks Chiamaka.

"Yes, I just... I don't know why Deriva hasn't entered the meeting room yet."

"I'm sure everything is fine. If they are having communication troubles, it may very well be affecting all of their comms."

I know she's trying to be comforting, but that isn't how Derivan technologies work. With multiple mechanisms powering our tech, it is very easy to bypass a fault in the system. For no one to be responding means either they don't want to respond or they cannot respond.

Prospects of the latter paint fear in my heart.

Meanwhile, the arguments escalate between the four present nations.

"Their goal is to take us down one by one..."

"Do you think they wouldn't hesitate to bomb us?"

As the dissent rises, Mirai's sights spin into action, and suddenly, our communication wires all shut off, making it so nothing we say can be heard over the virtual meeting room.

"Arguing will get us nowhere. We either unite as one to address this situation, or we will all fall to Seraphim control. Now..." She lifts a hand, and the light on Absko's microphone turns back on. "Shall we carry on this discussion like adults?"

But there's an interruption from Murasaki's monitor.

"A nautical from Deriva has just entered our borders. It is emitting a distress signal."

I sit up straighter in my seat. The point of view shifts to someone running down to the docks where, sure enough, a Derivan nautical has settled. It must be Kaito's sights we are seeing. The prince overrides the locking mechanism, and the hatch opens with a hissing pressure release. Inside is my brother, barely alive.

"Xipilli."

Chiamaka's hand grips my own. I didn't even realize how tightly I was holding onto the edge of my seat. The sensation only worsens when the other prince straps Wren's visor to his head and hits play. The video recording that plays in the visual scape of Murasaki's monitor is enough to tear my heart in two.

"This is Wren Nocturne of House Moctezumo. Technomancer ID#2787B65, reporting Cresta de Corail has fallen."

What does she mean? "Cresta de Corail has fallen." What is that supposed to mean? I turn back to my comm unit.

[Wren, what happened to xipilli? Where are you?]

No answer comes.

"My father, Vulcan Tlanextli, and Vulcana Elisabeta are dead. My brother, Crown Prince Xipilli Moctezumo, now Vulcan, is severely injured but alive and the sole survivor of the assault. I am setting an auto-piloted course for Shinka Temple with the hope that Empress Mirai and Murasaki no Yama, please, help my brother. My plan is to follow behind on my own, but in the event I am unable to, I request that whoever is watching this deliver a message to my brother and sister that I love them and will find them as soon as I am able. In the meantime, please, Miyazaki-heika, save my brother."

The message is dated from two days ago.

I can't believe what I'm hearing.

"Atzi?"

"Atzi, are you alright?"

"Princesa?"

People are calling my name. I know they are, I can hear them plain as day, but surely, they're talking to someone else. That's not me. I'm not Atzi. My whole world didn't just collapse on the other side of a computer monitor. No, all this has to be happening to some other poor, unfortunate soul.

"Atzi? Answer me."

I'm sure she would love to, Chike, but I don't know what the question is.

Instead, I run.

I run all the way to the stables. Tanzita is grazing outside. She is already saddled. Chike and I were supposed to go on another safari after the meeting. Happy to see me, she is quick to kneel for me, but instead of climbing into the passenger canopy, I settle behind her neck in the driver's seat. I've seen Chike do it enough.

"Yip, yip!"

Tanzita takes off at a jaunt.

"To the baobab tree."

I don't know why I want to go there. There was something about it. Something I need right now. I can't think. I can't breathe. The wind hits me hard in the face. It howls through the nearby trees and pulls my hair from its knot. The locks whip me in the face, over and over and over again until they begin to stick, glued to my skin by the tears trailing down my cheeks.

Papá... Mamá... Xipilli... Wren... All of the adepts of Cresta de Corail. The maids who made our beds, the wait staff who made sure our lives were as easy as possible, my teachers and tutors. All of them, gone with a simple word.

It doesn't make sense.

"Aziza."

Wren's smile was forced in that video. She was hurt and in pain and looked like she was in the middle of a battle for her life. No, wait. Not just her life. Xipilli's life. My poor brother. He looked as though he had been tortured by goddess knows what. His eyes. My god, his eyes were burned by something. I've only ever seen those kinds of burns in history books.

Those books recounted old war horrors of witches who used to pour acid into the eyes of their victims.

"Aziza."

Tanzita stops her cantor. We are here at the baobab tree. I don't even wait for the elephant to kneel. I simply jump off. I land hard, feet first then hands and elbows. There's blood on my knees and my dress is now torn, but the pain doesn't register. I get up and run to the tree.

"Aziza."

I hear my own voice whisper the word, but I don't know why it is falling from my lips. I don't even know what "Aziza" means. I just know that I have to say it. Don't ask me why.

The bark is rough on my bruised and torn palm. Thunder rumbles in the sky. That's right. Chike said the monsoon season would be coming soon.

"The rains have come early."

I hear the voice behind me, but when I look, nothing is there.

"Who is there?"

"How can I help you, pretty one? Please, let me help you. I'm sure I can make your wish come true if you but ask," the disembodied voice continues.

"I want my brother and sister back alive and safe."

The bark is rough against my lips. When did I press my face into the wood? It feels like pressing a kiss to Death's hands.

"Is that all, pretty one?"

"Yes, that's all I want. My siblings safe and sound."

"As you wish, pretty one. Just remember, there is a price for all things."

I close my eyes as the sky opens up. A sudden sharp pain in my naval brings me to my knees. It is like being punched in the gut, only deeper. Another jab rips the air from my lungs. A third hit, and the world ceases its rotation. I fall into a cold embrace.

All I'm aware of around me is the roar of Tanzita's trumpeting and the voice of the one I love calling my name.

10

Solemn Serenade

There isn't a word in the English language for the pain suffered in the loss of a pregnancy. We are expected to simply carry on as normal, even though our whole life has been turned topsy-turvy. Unable to sustain the most basic of human endeavors, it feels like our bodies have betrayed us. A tiny joy, so delicate, was snuffed out without even our say-so. Fear grips our hearts as the blood seeps into our clothes, and the doctors have so little care, they tell us to go bleed it out at home.

There should be a word for survivors of miscarriage.

Maybe it will help us understand how to deal with what has happened to us.

By Anonymous

Dawn of the Next Day

"WE DID EVERYTHING WE COULD, but I'm afraid the stress was too much for her body to handle."

Bright light sears into my eyes. I screw them shut again. "Atzi. My storm flower."

"Chike..."

"Yes, it's me. I'm here."

Warm hands wrap around mine. This time when I open my eyes, it isn't to blinding overhead lights but to the warm chestnut eyes of my husband.

"Thank the goddesses you are awake."

I move to sit up, but Chike stops me. "D-d-don't move. You've just been through a major ordeal."

"What happened? Where am I?"

"You're in the hospital, my love. After—after the news of Deriva, you ran off into the reserve. If it hadn't been for Tanzita making a riot, we may not have found you in time. The monsoons have come early this year."

"Princess Atzi." A woman comes over to my bedside. She is wearing purple medical scrubs and a blue surgical mask. "My name is Dr. Yang. I'm glad to see you are waking up. Do you feel any pain anywhere?"

Now she mentions it, my whole body aches in a variety of ways. My knees and elbows are throbbing. My back and neck ache. I feel more than a little light-headed. Worst of all, my stomach hurts something fierce, cramped up and tender as if I am having a really bad period.

She nods her head somberly as I tell her this. "That's to be expected, all things considered."

"What things?"

I look at Chike, who avoids my gaze.

"What things, doctor?"

"When your husband found you, you were bleeding profusely. We did everything we could to save the pregnancy, but I'm afraid your body just went into rejection syndrome."

"Wait, what does that mean? What happened to my baby?"

"I'm afraid you've suffered a miscarriage, your highness. The stress of hearing the fate of your family caused your body to suffer an adrenaline spike, and I'm afraid, as a result, you underwent what we call Spontaneous Ejection of Viable Embryo. Your body's stress response basically informed your uterus that having a baby was not a safe option right now and saw fit to terminate the pregnancy outright."

"But that's not right. My baby was healthy. My doctor said everything was in perfect order."

"Stress is deadly, your highness. Even the most healthy, full-term babies can end up stillborn if the stress response is not handled correctly."

"So my baby is dead?"

The doctor nods.

"I'm so sorry, my dear."

Stress caused me to have a miscarriage. (Aziza, Aziza, Aziza.) No, that's not right. (I wish ... for my brother and sister to be returned to me safe and sound.) I did this. The dream I had with the tiny fae. That was Aziza. That was her name. I made a deal with a fairy. (Everything comes with a price.) And as payment for holding up her end of the deal, she took my unborn.

"I've scheduled you for a psych consult. It's always a good idea to have a trauma assessment done after the loss of a pregnancy."

"So I don't go crazy."

"So you can manage your stress and avoid PTSD. You've already been through a tremendous trauma. We want you to be as healthy mentally as you are physically. You are very healthy still, physically. I imagine, if you wanted to, you and your husband could try again quite successfully for another pregnancy in six to seven weeks. You are young, and there was no lasting damage. It is simply up for you to decide whether you're ready to try again or not."

"I see."

Chike's thumb rubs the back of my hand.

"Could you give us a moment, doctor? I think my wife and I would like to mourn alone."

"Of course, your highness."

The door clicks shut behind her, leaving us alone.

"Chike?" I call.

"My love?" he answers.

"Is it true?"

The clock in the corner of the room only ticks five times before he answers, but to me, those five ticks took hours upon hours of time.

"Yes, Atzi. It's true. Deriva has fallen to Seraphim's forces."

The monsoon returns. This time it pours from my eyes.

"My father has declared war on Seraphim. As have all three of the other nations. We will avenge Deriva, Atzi. At whatever cost."

Chike's strength carries me through the storm. He holds me as I sob a never-ending river of pain and grief.

"Xipilli?"

"He is stable but has yet to wake. The Miyazaki family has extended us their hospitality as soon as we wish to be by his side."

I nod.

"We should go as soon as possible. My brother should not wake to strangers tending to him."

"As soon as you are ready for travel, we will go."

"What about Wren? Did she make it to Murasaki like she said she would?"

"There is no trace of her, Atzi. We are looking everywhere we can." No, not Wren. Not my baby sister. Lost and alone out there, wounded, probably mortally so. "Atzi, if it is the last thing I do, I will bring your sister back home."

I never thought it would be like this. Falling in love in the midst of a war. Grieving for loss while gaining everything else. Love will never fill the void of losing my parents. My brother's suffering will forever be my own. And my sister... my poor sister out there somewhere, lost, missing in action all because she put Xipilli's life before her own.

She had everything going for her. A career she was passionate about, talent in song and in battle, and a most recent surprising revelation, a budding romance with a young prince, something she always said she would never in a million years succumb to.

Then there is my unborn, a light snuffed out before it even had a chance to bloom.

"Atzi, I'm here for you. Whatever you need. I'm here for you."

At least, Chike is here with me.

"I know, *mi amor*. I know."

"I love you."

How can I tell him I betrayed him? How can I tell him that my deal with a fairy caused us to lose our child?

A Year and a Half Later – 28th Day in the Month of Storms 1963 A.P. – Orisumi

My hospital room this time is so much more comfortable. I could almost forget there is a war going on somewhere across the continent.

Not that such a thing matters right now. I have my own battle to win.

"Alright, princess. Now is the time. When I tell you, bear down as hard as you can and push. Ready, one, two, push!"

I follow the doctor's instructions. I push with all my might, gritting my teeth and bearing down as much as I can. Chike's hand in mine anchors me to the waking world. I've been in labor for more than half a day.

The epidural in my back has done its job well, and while I am uncomfortable, I am not in agonizing pain. I am able to enjoy the birth of my baby.

"Okay, relax."

I let go, panting into Chike's shoulder.

"You're doing so well, my love."

"Only because I have you here."

"I'm not going anywhere, Atzi. I've got you, and I've got our baby."

"Okay, princess. One more push. I can see your baby's head now. Ready, push!"

I give it my all and am rewarded with the piercing cries of a newborn.

"It's a girl."

Before I even have time to look down for my daughter, she is placed on my chest, a squirming, foam and fluid crusted bundle of new life. I can't believe it. She is the most beautiful thing I've ever seen.

"You did it, Atzi. You did it. Our little princess is earthside."

"She is, isn't she?"

I smile down at my screaming baby. Her APGAR scores are definitely going to be high. Good color, good size, good activity, good respiration. She's perfect. And no one will ever be able to tell me otherwise.

"Zenza Paloma Nagi, welcome to the world, baby girl."

Chike and I chose the name Zenza so that she could learn to count on her own inner strength. Paloma, I chose.

Nearly two years on from when my sister went missing, and I think about her every day, hoping and praying that my wish to the fae will come to fruition, yet we have heard nothing. Xipilli refuses to give up, but I have always been more practical than that. The chances of Wren returning to us by this point are none.

So I give my daughter the name Paloma, the Derivan name for dove. A songbird born for a songbird lost.

Welcome to the world, my little light. I wish you could have met your *tia*. Her voice could have moved mountains had she only had the chance.

Little did I know that in just two short months, my sister would return to me, changed forever.

Indexes

Glossary of Characters

By Faction

Deriva:
- Atzi Nagi nee Moctezumo – Princess of Deriva – Eldest daughter of Tlanextli and wife of Chike Nagi. Mother of Zenza Paloma Nagi.
- Elisabeta De Claré – Vulcana of Deriva – Mother of Atzi and Xipilli Moctezumo.
- Tlanextli Moctezumo – Vulcan of Deriva – Father of Atzi and Xipilli Moctezumo with his first wife, Elisabeta De Claré, and of Wren Nocturne with his second wife, Freya Nocturne.
- Freya Nocturne – Second Wife of Tlanextli Moctezumo – Firefly and Mother of Wren Nocturne.
- Xipilli Moctezumo – Current Vulcan of Deriva – 247th Trials Graduate – Atzi's younger brother.
- Wren Nocturne – Youngest child of Tlanextli Moctezumo – 247th Trials Graduate - Atzi's younger half-sister.

- Maria – Atzi and Wren's personal maid.
- Ebele:
- Absko Nagi – Orisha of Ebele – Father of Chike and Chiamaka Nagi
- Chike Nagi – Crown Prince of Ebele – 247th Trials Graduate – Husband of Atzi Moctezumo and Father to Zenza Nagi
- Chiamaka Nagi – Princess of Ebele – Younger sister to Chike Nagi and Zenza's paternal aunt.
- Tanzita – Chike's steed, a cybergean elephant.
- Kwame – Absko's biomechanical lion.

Notable Weapons of Deus:
- Mångata – Wren's Ætherkalis
- Agni – Chike's Blast Rifle

Glossary of Terms

- Adept – An augmented person equipped with military-grade technology. Certified to hunt and track hexen.
- Aziza – Beautiful benevolent fairies of West African myth often depicted as small pretty women.
- Deriva – An island country within the League, Deriva is home to a constitutional monarchy led by the Vulcan
- Cyborg – An augmented person possessing a set minimum of technological enhancements, or a human+ possessing enhancements essential to their ability to live (i.e. respiratory life support, mechanical hearts, spinal augmentations to prevent paralysis).
- Elokoi – A trickster fae of Ebele. They often pretend to be aziza to gain the trust of unsuspecting humans.
- Fae – Fairy Folk – Magical creatures that pre-date witchcraft in Deus. The Fae generate their own wild magic and live independently of witches. (Examples of Fae in Deus: Pixies, Nymphs, Mermaids, Trolls.)

- Firefly – A person who devotes their life to serving at the pleasures of others. They are performers, musicians, storytellers, and often times people of the sexual arts.
- Hexen – The Spell Folk – Magic users and creatures reliant on or resultant of witchcraft. (Examples of Hexen: Witches, Werewolves, Vampyres, Goblins.)
- Human+ – A person who accepted technology into their existence via a permanent integration. This can be as mediocre an augmentation as a cochlear implant or as extensive as a prosthetic limb or neural net.
- Technomancer – A League-certified human+ capable of channeling energy through their technology. Technomancers are specially trained and equipped to hunt and kill dangerous fae, hexen, undead, and other magical creatures. Their augmentations are top-of-the-line and require an immense amount of discipline to maintain and control.
- Witch – A practitioner of witchcraft, the act of molding and utilizing wild magic to effect change in the outer world. Witches in Deus achieve their powers and abilities through a mixture of blood-inheritance and practical study and are considered the most dangerous of beings as the practice of unrestricted magics can lead to psychological breakdown and magic fever.

Book Club Questions

1. What resemblances did you see between Atzi and Chike's wedding and how we know royal weddings are conducted in real life?
2. What do you think of Atzi's relationship with her various family members?
3. Would you be able to go through with an arranged marriage? Why or why not?
4. What are your thoughts about the relationship between Atzi and her sister?
5. What do you think of Atzi as a character as she grows throughout the story?
6. If you could imagine any celebrity as Chike, who would it be and why?
7. How would you have reacted to what Chike said to Atzi in Chapter 6? Do you think he deserved a good wallop or did Atzi overreact?
8. Did Atzi make the wrong decision?
9. How does your opinion of Chike change as the story progresses?
10. Do you think Atzi took Absko up on the option of having Ebelean tech implanted into her body?

About the Author

LYRA R. SAENZ IS A WRITER OF SCIENCE Fiction/Fantasy. A romantic at heart with a love for supernatural horror, she believes that while happy endings don't come easily, they do come, even if it means excising your ex into a glass jar.

Born and raised in South Texas, Lyra is a multicultural, eyeliner-wielding member of the LGBTQ+ community, an animal-lover, and a cynic of all things political. She presently haunts the Houston area with her amazingly supportive partner and her feline-shaped void, Violet. Lyra grew up bouncing between her Chicano and Scandinavian heritages never feeling like she really fit in one world or the other.

Despite growing up on enchiladas and lefsa, she'll never turn down an offering of sushi or pho. And while her friends were getting boyfriends and girlfriends, she was too busy crushing on dreamy anime and manhwa characters to bother with real people. So with one foot on either side of the border and her head full of East-Asian pop culture, she started creating her own worlds.

A lover of all things witchy, paranormal, and ghostly with a side of Victorian-futurism, cyberpunk, and posthumanism, Lyra imagines worlds where the IT tech is a werewolf and the coffee machine has a fairy living inside it but the androids love to take walks down the forest trail and host the occasional bonfire. When she isn't lost somewhere between an inkwell and a notebook, she can be found acting as a throne for the real queen of the household -Her cat and her royal majesty demands snuggles constantly. Or sitting and listening to her partner play video games while she unsuccessfully knits and/or binges her latest international tv show.

More books from
4 Horsemen Publications

Romance

Fantasy, SciFi, & Paranormal Romance

Amanda Fasciano

Waking Up Dead
Dead Vessel
The Dead Show
Dead Revelations

Beau Lake

The Beast Beside Me
The Beast Within Me
Taming the Beast: Novella
The Beast After Me
Charming the Beast
The Beast Like Me
An Eye for Emeralds
Swimming in Sapphires
Pining for Pearls

Chelsea Burton Dunn

By Moonlight
Moonbound
Bloodthirsty

D. Lambert

Rydan
Celebrant
Northlander
Esparan
King
Traitor
His Last Name

Danielle Orsino

Locked Out of Heaven
Thine Eyes of Mercy
From the Ashes
Kingdom Come
Fire, Ice, Acid, & Heart
A Fae is Done

J.M. Paquette

Klauden's Ring
Solyn's Body
The Inbetween
Hannah's Heart
Call Me Forth
Invite Me In
Keep Me Close
Heart of Stone

Kait Disney-Leugers

Antique Magic
Blood Magic

Kyle Sorrell

Munderworld
Potarium

Lyra R. Saenz

Prelude
Falsetto in the Woods: Novella
Ragtime Swing
Sonata

Discover more at
4HorsemenPublications.com

www.ingramcontent.com/pod-product-compliance
Lightning Source LLC
Chambersburg PA
CBHW020233120726
47903CB00008B/2652